YOU KNOW I'M HAPPY

EMBRACE THE GLORIOUS MESS

ARYA

To my four-legged friend Pogo.

We miss you.

Contents

CHAPTER ONE

It was raining on the roadways, and you could feel the dampness on your feet. The air was made moist by the nocturnal rain. That has the potential to awaken your creative spirit while also inducing purposeful slumber. You can wear anything in Mumbai because of its tropical, wet, and dry environment. Typically, the temperature is moderately high and the humidity is high. Tropical climates and coastal environments guarantee little temperature variation. Rain, though, is a another story.

Manya realizes she has made a mistake once more when she looks at the wall clock at nine in the morning. On her first day of college, she is untimely. She was composed in some way, but her father was not pleased with her actions. He was knocking on the door nonstop. When she's asleep, she prefers a dead corpse, and she wakes up when she feels it's time. She did dress simply, wearing blue trousers and a white T-shirt with the word "NO" on it. She doesn't want to make sense, but it also doesn't make sense.

She remembered school well. Though college was somewhat different and many of her friends travelled overseas or out of town for college, she was still able to make a large number of friends. She seemed to be the only person who would be in the same city. This reassures her repeatedly about her decision. She must remain nevertheless in order to pursue her acting profession. Although her father never expressed it to her, he detested it in the back of his mind. He was cool with theatre school because he knew she would never listen. If she makes living from it, everything is fine to him.

Manya look back to see the time, which is 9:47 a.m. She is a little—no, a lot—slow. She was terrified, but she never showed it in her behaviour. The father-daughter pair are both at ease. Manya is actually experiencing a bit of a mental wave between her college and school years. She enjoyed being well-known in school, but now she don't knows what to do at college. Because of her online persona, she was concerned that people would make fun of her. In essence, she aspired to be both, top and well-known. Using her phone, she shot a picture in the kitchen, posing in a victorious stance and wearing a false smile. She shared a narrative on social media. She took ten seconds to look at the picture. Her father gazed at her for ten seconds, curious about her activities. Then she instantly removed it. He simply gave a nod of his head and carried on reading his paper. Ready for the day, he was. He receives a bungalow with all the amenities because he is an Indian administrative service official, but he makes sure that her daughter doesn't feel alone. In order to live next door to his childhood buddy Arif Ji, he makes an effort to buy an apartment. It is not good for her to be alone; she needs company. As he also wanted surrounded by people. He go back and forth.

The bell rung. Manya remained in her house. To determine who will open the door, they both glance at one another. Interestingly, Manya was the one. "Good morning," said an intrigued Danish, followed by Manya. He gives Manya a lunch box. "I made vadapav for you." She said without thanking him. "Dude, you're running a little late." She refused to let him inside.

Eventually, Manya's father broke the stillness in the morning, saying, "I think it's you who are late". Her peculiar morning ritual was too much for him to cling to. All she could say was "Yeah, yeah." Far too grave. "Actually, I agree with you, however I arrived late with the lunchbox a little later than expected". He says, "Sorry about that," focusing on the lunchbox. Even though he knew he wasn't welcome today, he did clear the path. "I am no longer a child," she declares. He didn't respond, and instead of giving him the time, she hurried off with her lunchbox and bag in such a hurry that she didn't even hear them say goodbye wishes. Now that she was gone, her father could finally relax. Danish stood there grinning, as if he could make sense of her words. It might never come to pass.

She took Tok-Tok because she had plans despite the terrible traffic in Mumbai. Then went to the college by foot. She was rushing so much as she walked in. Compare oneself to everyone and analyse them so fast. Beautiful faces, flawless makeup, and a perfect body. Everything appeared to Manya to be in opposition to her, yet consistent with her online character. She dashes back towards her department as soon as she discovers she arrived from the wrong side. Although the college offers many other programs, its drama school is its most well-known feature. Manya entered on her first try, despite the fact that it appears to be difficult. She felt even more assured about her work as a result, although she was still wary of challenges. She was aware that there would be pupils more skilled than her. Additionally, she won't feel comfortable in the competition.

After seeing the "Mumbai Art and Drama School" board, she felt a little better but uneasy about approaching the teacher. Manya needs to implement what she thinks. She turned to face the sound of voices as she hurried toward the orientation ceremony that she had noticed. When she arrived at class, everyone was occupied with conversation. She ponders for a moment after that. After her, a boy turned. "In what batch?" Among the students, he looked curious as he asked. It seemed to him that she was perplexed. However, Manya want help from anyone but orientation ceremony slipped her mind. Despite the high humidity in the air, he smells rather good, which is why she is examining him. Alright, she is also able to smell the money. "I am actually a fresher; where is the ceremony for orientation?" she was awake up by his handsomeness. The truth sinks in. Though he was a little bewildered, he smiled. A very cute smile for her. He pointed to the board that lists the day and said, "I think you missed it; it was yesterday." While nobody was intrigued, a lot of strange conjecture caught people's attention. Everyone chuckled at that. The boy managed to hang on, though. It was only Manya who felt let down. As she approached the board, she noticed Day, her error, and her carelessness. Behind her was that guy. Calmly, he said, "It's okay; you're still a student at this college." Manya believed he was correct.

In defiance of her better judgment, she selected the class. Everyone was grinning when she walked in, and she grinned back. She thinks about her seating arrangement. Everybody has selected a seat. That guy motioned for everyone else to move to the side. Without giving it much thought, she sat next to him.

"What's your name," His eyes gave off the impression that he was staring at her.

"Ah Manya," the dismay girl said, growing tense.

As they shook hands, he insisted, "I am Yash."

It seemed a little too innocent to her. But you alter on the outside in the hopes of finding favour. She doesn't have a lot of faith. She opened her backpack and removed the lunch box. and begin your meal.

"Would you like some?" She said, trying to be kind.

"I had my breakfast," he graciously declined.

"Oh, okay, good for me," she said, perhaps half-teasing, half-joking. Just Manya is aware.

"Why, do you not post these days?, I already follow you on social media," he replied. She was shocked to learn why he was acting that way.

"Why?" She had vadapav in her mouth when the teacher entered, so she was unable to say much.

There's something about Manya that draws the teacher in so fast. "Why you are eating in my class?" As soon as he walked into the classroom, the teacher asked her. She felt stuck, not knowing what to say to Yash and the teacher. "I have a broad range of experience." Feeling enraged, he responds, "Miss you cannot fool me." Everyone was anticipating her response. "I am not making any fool; I just missed my breakfast," she gulped and seemed to be innocent. "Oh, I don't care," he responded, taking the package and walking over to her seat. And add trash while acting as if nothing occurred. Feeling a little down. With a little chuckle, he said, "Your mom must be furious because he threw your box." However, she considered the words he would use to address her mother is for Danish. She was a little embarrassed by herself on the first day. But there was nothing she could do. She therefore seated still in class, not any movement, no any trouble. "You don't have a pen?." He was the only one who found it enjoyable. He passed this strange-looking pen. Manya paused, but her gaze remained fixed on the pen. It was child-like in its colour. Writing with it wasn't convenient.

"I don't have pen, I don't have mind, I can't remember a day and now don't my tiffin also." a lot of pain but still managed to smile. "Why do you act weird?" she uttered without glancing at him. "Not more strange than you," he remarked.

She leaves the room first after the lesson ends. She felt ashamed; it was understandable that she had forgotten her orientation day, but she was going mad from feeling like the class idiot. She was in such a rush that she neglected to give Yash back the pen. She seek out immediately. Still longing for food. Continued to fantasize about eating. Finding the canteen was easy than department for her. She entered the canteen directly; it had a standard interior with little decor, simply a counter where food is served and a table and chair that were normally used but were empty today. She started by looking through the board-mounted menu, which included several options. A man approached from the back and said, "Don't be fooled, it is just for show; they have only one dish, a vegetarian plate." There was silence in the air. Manya ignored him and placed her own order. Yet felt a little disappointment. Truly, she murmured regretfully. "We have tea as well," the counter man who was filling the kullad cup with tea added. When he offered Manya as well, she turned him down. "Any non-vegetarian dish," Manya manages to hold onto some hope. He was suddenly very irate and said, "We have only vegetarians; you want it or not." Manya grabbed them because she was hungry even though she had no other options. It moved so quickly. The plate was ready when the counter man handed it to Manya. Surprised by the speed, she said, "So fast."

"They possess just one item from this menu; it's not that anything unaware; it will happen quickly," the man who had forewarned Manya continued to be present. Perhaps he was getting drama for the day since he was bored with his day. After accepting the platter, she sat down. The man trailed her to the chair as well. He looked sincere as he replied, "Maybe you didn't notice me; I am also in your class." He was staring at the door all the time. She speculated, "Are you waiting for friends?" Sad, not into her at all. "Yes," he grinned. Despite her unhappiness with the cuisine, she continued to eat in the hopes of staying healthy.

"Whoa," Yash suddenly appeared, looking for someone. Numerous was it.

"Where were you?, I was looking for you.," "Kartik, why are you here?," he sat there right away, full of questions. He seems like a friend. Manya enquired of Kartik. "No, he is your friend," Kartik says, clearly not feeling fond of Yash. He doesn't appear to like him, nor does Yash. When they watched Manya devour the entire thing, they both forgot. "Why do you consume such garbage?," Yash was taken aback. Kartik said, "You must be hungry from the days." He was repulsed. Kartik's friends arrived and took a seat with him. There was only one female other than her, who gave her a look. They all having a chat when she notice her.

"What's your name?" alone she was eating which made her unease.

"Manya."

"Hi there, I'm Niti." Shoved the other guy.

"Shresth," he said with a smile.

Manya had no idea that she would be able to make friends on her first day. She felt a little pins and needles after the humiliation. She is aware that the career she has choice can be polished when she interact. You discover more about human nature's traits and tendencies the more you converse. The more she interact with people will understand the craft of observation and acting. And the theatre can provide her with the live experience which she is missing. However, she was scared to take action without direction.

Niti spotted Manya earlier on social media and said, "I have seen you." That was her point. Little Manya was so uncomfortable that she was identified by others. She was lying when she said, "Yeah, I do it sometime in my free time, just like everybody else does these days." She really like how social media allows her to be recognized and reach millions of people. We'll see, though, that she can maintain probity. While everyone else was chatting, Yash and Manya were silent. Manya received no opportunity to contribute, and Yash was not interacting with anyone. It appears that Kartik, Niti, and Shresth are getting along well. Kartik tells Manya to eat outside of the campus; the food there is more superior. Yash teases, "You can try the vadapav." Each person laughed aloud.

Yash said, "I have to go because I have theatre practice," but no one seemed to care.

Manya was taken aback and said, "Oh, you started earlier than us; I am doing only Kathak."

Kartik disagreed, saying, "No, I am also doing; in fact, I think everyone is doing maybe." "Everyone here should prepare themselves earlier; if you really want to do this, you should start as well." Shresth said calmly. She also realizes that she is living a very late life. Occasionally, you may take the initiative and think you are the first, but when you take a step forward, you will see that you are still behind. Cliché but it's works. However, it's not too late. Manya was contemplating joining any club in depth. Then acknowledge that she has to leave for the celebration. Because tomorrow is her best buddy Danish's birthday. Her plan was to surprise his friend—who she didn't really think would happen.

"I actually can't go to any theatre today because I have a party planned. Can you guys please assist me tomorrow?," Manya concluded that it would be best to request help. "Yes," all of them concurred. She turned to go like a warrior who just conquer a tasteless, saltless, everything less dish. Yash follows her to watch her as she stands. Manya gave him no resistance. He trailed behind her.

Yash explained his lack of speech when they left the group, saying, "Actually, Kartik and I had a weird fight on the first day." "What may I ask for?" Manya started to wonder about the rumours. She getting late but gossip in few second wouldn't harm. "He believes that I was admitted based on merit, but in reality, I applied on my own, I gave interview also like others. On the orientation day, you can't imagine what he was subtly implying.

He sounded furious and literally fight in front of teacher that I got it some contacts."

"This is what he actually did," she exclaimed, startled.

"And then he starts fighting," he said, but was cut off as Manya's phone rang. She chose. "Oh, I'm on my way..., coming," she hurriedly said. "I apologize; I'm in a hurry. I'll see you tomorrow," she said as she hurried to the gate. Yash wished they could have spoken longer, but it was not possible. That he had forgotten to get her number, dawned on him.

She considered decorating her apartment, but then realized it would be in his flat would be better. She didn't decorate in a mature manner, to be sure. It was stuffed with vibrant ribbon and balloons. Not only that, but she also remembered the balloon stuffed with candy. Although Manya always tries to make his birthday special, Danish wasn't all that thrilled about it. Not quite, though. The party gives her too much energy. She had teased him with candles when she was younger, but Danish wasn't too fond of her. He exacts revenge by smashing the cake in her face after becoming enraged. Quiet yet powerful. Since he never ends up like the female she picks, Manya always tries to pair him up with any random girl she likes. He can't do this, in her opinion. Once his parents caught Danish which cause a lot stir in the house, he doesn't feel guilty. But this time, Manya received a reprimand. Danish claims she made him do it. In actuality, Manya was quieter than Danish. Although she was once a renegade, the Danish always triumphed over the Manya. As an adult, he developed a slight seriousness. His room is where he spends all of his time studying and coding. He achieved success at an early age. He put the other thing out of his mind and gave his studies a lot of attention. Though he was close to finishing his degree in software engineering, he continued to labour for pay. His triumph in working for large corporations without a degree is that he doesn't spend much because he wants to buy a car. He motivates Manya to put in a lot of effort in her life in some way. But surprisingly they never took each other as a competitor.

His friends were arriving one by one. Despite Manya's father lack of enthusiasm for wishing at 12:00 AM, his parents continued to encourage Manya. When her dad doesn't wake up, she gives up on getting him to come. When Danish takes off his headphones, he can hear everyone in the room talking, "They think it's a surprise," he sniff. He was able to hear everyone's voice. They were noisy, so he was speculating about the guest list, but he didn't sap their enthusiasm. Permit them to think it's a surprise.

Manya learns that the cake she made especially for him is missing. It was a home bakery of her friend. "I'm sorry to call at this time, hello." With grace, she attempted to persuade her, "I forgot the cake," she tried to be gentle as she can. "Did you see the time, you my friend? But friendship has its ups and downs," said the friend who wasn't all that great. She was not persuaded. "I'm sorry, I was overloaded. I simply ignored that". As of 11:20 p.m. She could attend on time. She may extend her apology farther. But she was won over the baker.

Everyone was there, but many people asked if they might have the cake. Still she wanted her cake to be main. It was then she decided to travel alone. She got into her father's private vehicle. She turned on the music first, got to the desired location. She quickly picked up the cake that her grumpy, exhausted friend had handed her. Manya was perplexed as to why she went to bed so early. She is not a member of her generation. She was inside the allotted time. She was moving along rather smoothly when a dog crossed the road in the centre. She became a little worried and lost control of the vehicle. She veered to the right and crashed the vehicle into the partition. The car wasn't in a position to go any farther, and she was acting appropriately. She felt as though her hands were trapped somewhere, and she became aware that there was agony there that she was fainted. She's able to pick up on whispers of the crowd surrounded her. She was becoming less sensible.

"Happy birthday," everyone exclaimed aloud. It pleased Danish parents to see their child flourish. Danish did appear taken aback—not by the party, but rather by the number of people and the décor, felt nostalgic about the 1990s. Everyone was happy for him. Grinning, he expresses gratitude for everything. He intended to get a cake cut. He was ready to extinguish the candles. "Where's Manya at?". It bothered him in an odd way. Everyone was looking her over but didn't find. Drunker try to find her under the table. She simply existed the entire time. He did really hear her. One individual commented, "She went to get the cake, but she didn't came back yet." Danish parents were more anxious. When they first called, she didn't pick up. Danish checked the location by opening his phone. Thank goodness it was showing. It stood in the centre of the street. Weird. Maybe she was driving.

Danish got into the car and went looking for her. Since she had been in the middle of the road for so long, he was suspicious and didn't want to consider the practical side of things. From far he could see crowd close to divider. He was getting apprehensive. Still he gathered all the courage. And run towards the car. She wasn't making sense, but he could see the car smashed from the front and the people attempting to assist her. He led her into his vehicle. Quickest he could do. Didn't even let emotion halt him. Her blood was quite thick. He was hardly able to see her clearly. Only things he know at that point to get hospital as soon as possible. All his way he tried to call her up. Loudly calling her name.

When he got to the hospital. He gave her father a call. Although she wasn't seriously hurt, she was on the road for a while and blood was flowing freely. Her head and hand were injured. Her father is a fearful man. There was just too much for him to handle. Even though she had broken hand, still he was pleased to learn that she was okay. She was alright. Enrolled in the ward. With everyone now at ease, they contemplated the potential outcomes. Bringing the situation to the realization that Manya's complete ignorance would be the cause or maybe phone.

Danish said, "Maybe the brakes fail; I will sent the car to be repaired." Manya's father was fairly certain that she was using her phone—no other car even seemed to have hit it. "I believe you are correct," Danish concurred. With a sensible remark, the Danish mother said, "I think we should wait; she can tell better." Still everyone anxiety was growing about the issue. Her eyes finally opened. The first thing she noticed was a dark TV screen mounted on the wall in front of her. She opened it slowly. She pondered. Though she wasn't even trying, she is able to speak.

Everyone then encircles her to observe her actions.

"How come you are not speaking?, maybe she lost her speak," A suspect from Danish. Happy but sad. "I'm not sure," Manya said, seeming dejected. "I was wrong". Not that she was screaming in agony but still couldn't bear it. "How did this come to be?" Her father was more interested in learning how it occurred. It took her a little while to speak. She was too fatigued to talk, but she was gathering her strength. "It was a dog, not what you might be thinking". Her voice was still low, "I thought I hit him, but the car slit, I couldn't control it, hit the divider." Danish began to grumble, "I can't believe I taught you to drive and you are so irresponsible."

"Oh, I'm at the hospital," she replies, continuing to assume that something has happened.

Not losing his cool, he remarked,

"You are changing the topic."

She said, "You teach me that's why it happens," and closed her eyes right away. She attempted to toss the drip bottle next to her to hit him, but she was unsuccessful. He was taught to behave more responsibly by his parents, who stopped him from acting like a youngster. Allow her to rest. Which was necessary took place. Everyone sat quietly, not really resting there. The incident causes them all to become frightened. The space was silent. These messages were only appearing on Danish phones.

"Are you able to silence your phone?," Danish's father became agitated.

"All right, that's not me doing it; it was just a birthday wish for me."

With strictness, he urged, "Just keep it silent."

"Happy birthday, I apologize for forgetting," Manya tried to stood up and wished him. It dawns on everyone that they have forgotten his birthday in the midst of everything. But now the festive vibe has completely faded. "Is there cake for us?" As she lay in bed, her gaze scanned the space. Danish turned around to discover the cake was not in good shape. Everything in the car was taken by him. He then brought it to the hospital. Taking the box, he sat down next to Manya.

"This already smashed, I don't think we cut it," Manya said with a dejected expression.

"Don't even try to eat this," he screamed in disgust.

With much grace, she says, "Can you give the candle?." With Danish's assistance, she lights the candle in her right hand—the only hand that functions at this time—saying, "Make a wish and blow it." And the candle was shattered. He followed her advice without protesting. Everyone joined her as she began to sing the birthday song. Strange, but it worked for her.

"Thank you; all right." Danish was finished granting additional wishes, saying, "Now we should go home; not everyone can stay here, You remain here; tomorrow we have our office," the Arif ji stated. And everybody concurred. In the second, Manya dozed off once more. He agreed, but he wanted to go to sleep. He's not interested in arguing. With one request, "Mom, come early in the morning," he spoke.

❧❧❧

Danish slumbered on the couch, which caused him some discomfort. He was constantly shifting back and forth, but he managed to adjust. She was in agony. "Danish, call the nurse; she can give me painkillers." When the nurse arrived, she was ruthless. She answered, "I'll give if it gets worse." Manya was furious that the nurse was holding off on making things worse. She had stopped sleeping and was now awake. "How did you discover me?" She was now curious to find out how it had occurred. Due to his frequent sleep, he apologized, saying, "I am not in mid-night chat mood." "I would want to ask you a question; would you please just respond to it?'" she exclaimed, getting louder. "Okay, I found you at your live location; on the day you said you had to go to school for paperwork but you came late, I know where you went; once you send, but you didn't set a timer for restriction, and it shows me always the right place; see, it is so good; maybe you are feeling betrayed, but show how it helped out a lot," he said, clearing everything up right away. However, Manya felt deceived. Danish waited for her response, but she remained silent.

It dawned on him that she was fast asleep. He didn't annoy her. Perhaps now she was feeling better. Any sound startled Manya into wakefulness. When she seen Danish lying on the ground covered by a blanket, she began to speculate about what it may be. How rapidly the night changes, she thought, horrified by what they were getting up to. After rising up and organizing himself, he remarks, "It's easy when you have a good bed."

"Oh my god, I could have died," she continued to reflect on herself.

"You can murder someone, but not yourself. But why are you talking about death this morning?" He was back on the couch. He muttered, "Ah, when mom will come," before turning in for the sleep. Several attempt to get out of bed. When he notices her, he also stands up. She proceeded to the restroom. Now she was better. The only things hurting were her right hand and a few cuts. She returned from the restroom. Manya sat on the sofa and said, "Now you want my sofa too." He was exhausted. She was serious when she said, "You can sleep on my bed anytime your mother will come, and maybe I can go home now." He felt as though he was there and had no choice but to stare at the bed at first. After working all day after her accident, he was exhausted. How he yearned to sleep.

"Who are you?" the bewildered nurse asked.

"I apologize; I am not the patient. She is over there," he said, gesturing to the couch where she was straining to eat an apple. Without delay, he rose from the bed.

Manya said "Hello," but the nurse didn't reciprocate.

"This is what?," She said, "I can complain to the doctor; it's for the patient," in an unfriendly manner. But it was wrong also. "Well, I did insist. Oh, I see. What's the big deal?, I am being let go today," she asked honestly. The nurse regarded her strangely. She gave food and lot of medicine. And then requested to Danish for discharge paperwork following the doctor's appointment. They were both relieved when she went. Danish sampled some idli sambhar, but found it too bland. They awaited the return of someone. They gazed at the door, like kids. At last, Danish's mother arrived at the hospital. Seeing that his mother could finally return home and be free of this strange hospital odour gave her a sense of stress. She couldn't wait to take a bath.

CHAPTER TWO

After a month

"Would you please prepare breakfast today?" The Danish's father was eager to get to work. Danish took up an onion-chopping task instead. Began getting everything ready for Poha. He moved pretty fast. However, he had a search in mind. In an attempt to assist, his mother said, "What you want." While he was still looking, he said, "A lunch box that I have; it's keeps the food warm." She handed him the second box and added, "You gave that one to Manya."

Suddenly it sparked in his mind. In the playground area, he spotted Manya swinging in the society ground. He headed there right away. "Why do you not enrol in college?" The swing was moving quickly, but children were lined up at the back, waiting for their turn. She stays silent. This appears unprofessional. "Get up, kids, they're watching," he said, embarrassed.

One of the children announced to the group, "5 minutes are up."

"All right," Manya said, giving them a seat right away.

Her actions had become tiresome to him. She said to him, "Actually, I am not in the mood right now," without saying anything else. "Go to college; you are wasting your time, this is what you argue about with your dad about," he stated gravely. "I consider it," On the steps, Manya was leaping. They entered her room. Danish was trailing her as well. Seeing the Yash pen on her desk, he teases, "When you will return this pen to your devotee." She's spent a lot of days in her house. Her room is really disorganized. She said, "I will return it when I go," without taking offense. She took a poster and stuck it on the wall by her desk. "Don't be a part of it problem, be the entire problem." She took it pretty seriously. "For what kind of purpose is it?" He was never able to understand her. She point at him. It's for him.

"I am here doing this; everyone is ahead of me; I haven't even completed my kathak classes or posted anything on social media," she exclaims. She took a photo of the desk and uploaded it to social media. He was ready to go.

With a scowl, she said, "I can upload the hospital pictures."

"All right, really, where's my lunch box?" He refused to go until he had the response.

"It is somewhere on Earth," she asserted with assurance.

"Where exactly do I want to know right now, on earth?"

She grinned and said, "It's somewhere, but I don't know where yet. I'll let you know when I do."

Taking a deep breath, he made the decision to give up.

❧❧❧

"What are you up to?" Manya had been up to something, and this morning her father was observing her. She was getting ready to go to college when she ultimately made the decision. Her attention span is long. She is inherently sluggish. She grabbed a backpack and filled it with clothes and her gungaru for her kathak classes. The bell was rung by the maid. Quickly she came. She was preparing their morning meal, aloo paratha. Manya ate her breakfast first. She kept silent. A list of all she needs to get done in a day. Her father didn't eat breakfast, so she gave him the lunch box.

"Do I have to drop?" her father enquired.

"No," she immediately replied. She believes that bringing her dad along will be awkward. You have to look good and cool for your age. Adolescents imitate the styles that adults adopt, setting an example for the rest of society. But she was going through a crisis of identity. Although she was fabricating herself so that others would not criticize her, she does not currently have any problems. Yash liked her story about returning to college right away when she uploaded it. "He something," she began to suspect.

She was walking through the gate as she entered the campus. The security halted her. "Where is your ID?" inquired the guard. Manya was working on something for two hours, but she forgot the ID. Nothing is beneficial to her. She looked through the entire purse, but she didn't find any cards. Watching her intently, the guards were hoping she would give. The other guard motioned for her to go and try again. "Why would someone get dressed up in the morning to attend college? Someone could be an idiot," she reasoned, hoping they would overlook her.

"Really, you think," he remarked, appearing displeased by her remark. She thought about providing them a receipt for the fee. She benefited from their acceptance of the fee receipt. "Get the ID; it's mandatory," he cautioned her. She try to smile.

She proceeded directly to the theatre. It was her class; a girl was on the stage, and everyone was seated around the teacher. He was discussing the stage's placement. And Yash sees her. He appeals to her in silence, "Come here." Her seat was next to his. She was taking notes while paying attention to the talk. To get practical, the instructor summons a group of students. He gave a brief, teasing peek of drama. It caused Manya to focus on girls instead of boys. The girl appears to be an established actor already. She continued to stare at her even after they had all completed the lesson. Manya came to take the front seat as the class was adjourning. The females and a few more students were still on stage, creating a circle in the middle and showcasing their talents.

"Wow, she looks amazing," Manya remarked quietly.

"Why are you swooning over her when she's fine?" Yash heard her. On her left side, he was seated.

"She's all right!," Kartik said, "She's perfect,"on the right side.

"She is a kathak dancer in reality, and as you can see, she has grace and does excellent acting. She could advance in her career, in my opinion". Her beauty had mesmerized Kartik.

"It's just that you really like her, which is why you find everything positive," But Yash disagreed.

She declared, "I am a kathak dancer as well," with pride. No one cares.

"Perhaps you don't have enough grace," Kartik said firmly.

"Pay no attention to him," Never did Yash agree to Kartik. It was unclear to her who she should pay attention to.

Kartik said, "She received the highest number for admission."

She inhaled deeply.

"Her name?" she enquired of her rival.

"Mansi" stated it simultaneously. Kartik, though, more firmly.

Taking out her phone, Manya searched for her on social media. It was a relief for her that Manya had more followers than she had, even though she was well-known on social media. She kept silent. Nonetheless, she couldn't stop wondering how she wouldn't be superior to her. She was trying to convince herself that she was not perfect. Nobody is able to be humble and flawless at the same time. Since she is intelligent and gifted, she comes to the conclusion that she must at least possess attitude. Not until today, she noticed it. It was simply Manya's sense of inadequacy.

Kartik says, "Yeah, I want to date her, but it would be so fast."

With a scornful tone, she remarked, "You are a quick lover."

He declared, "I'm not doing it now; I'll see the best time."

As one class had to make way for another, everyone began exiting the auditorium. They were therefore going. And then, when they approached, Mansi went outside to open the door for the teacher. A suggestion of "Oh no, she is humble too" aggrieve she was feeling. Despite acting as though she didn't care, she was going insane. Although she can only maintain her sanity for five minutes, her inner self believes she is the greatest. A person with greater talent make other nervous. Manya know herself well that she couldn't tolerate competition but end up getting herself hurt. Jealousy, jealousy.

While preparing tea, Niti asked, "How is your hand now?" Everybody had a tea break over this. The following class is theirs. They thus don't want to overlook that one. "It seems to be ideal now," she remarks, trying not to focus on the agony. Manya realizes she left the pen behind. She handed it to Yash after taking it out of the bag. Yash felt horrible and said, "Oh, you keep it; sorry, I didn't come to meet you in the hospital." He wanted to but his overthinking didn't allow him. However, Yash was able to find the solution through contacting social media.

"What transpired with you?" The fact that she doesn't attend college never really bothers Kartik or Shresth.

"I met to an accident due to my stupidity," she replied, determined not to repeat the events.

Shresth felt horrible also, saying, "We only met you once; that's it; we didn't get to our minds."

Manya hesitated in the middle, "The good news is," and everyone watched to see what she would say next. "I am alive," she said, not finding it funny.

This month, she's not feeling well at all. Since Manya has lived with pain her entire life, she does not suffer many injuries. God had different ideas, but she was prepared for college. She is constantly concerned that she would fall behind and never achieve contentment. She has to be happy for herself before anybody else can, but for some reason, everyone around her father, Danish, and his family is tired of trying to make her as happy as they can. She grew a little quiet during the course of the month, but she is gathering herself to be herself. They inquire about her health since it both annoys her and the fact that she didn't connect with many people.

Manya wondered why Kartik had told her in private, "Today I will try out a act."

"So, what ought to I do?" She was perplexed.

"Let her be the protagonist," he asked.

"Like how can I do that?" She showed no interest.

He reassured, "Just listen to me; it will happen."

The teacher addressed Manya, saying, "It's your first day; I've never seen you before." He brought up the character's name. "Well, it's the second day," she said, fearing that he would chastise her. It was unexpected that he didn't trouble her, as he only accepts honest students. He says, "What role can you do?" Her gaze swerved to see Kartik. With a slight pause, she said, "I think negative will be good." She was thinking that he might say no. But he accepted. Additionally, she believe that was a lovely observation of her because actually the character quite fit her. The teacher always let other to choose the character. For better understanding. Still when someone deliberately force her she don't want it. Her heart broke over this. Childish. This was for her. Kartik seemed content. She was baffled by how he handled everything. However, he got what he desired. Upon seeing Mansi, her perspective changed. Possibly she's developed friendship with him.

Teaching is the art of reading a character and delving into their innermost thoughts. "How far away are you looking?" The instructor noticed that Manya was not paying attention. "Nothing," she apologize. She had been reading about her personality and character. "Why do you seem so lost?, What is causing you any trouble? Are feeling well?," Yash spoke. "Maybe, but not really," she said in a similar tone. "Don't worry; everything will be alright," they both grinned.

She was nevertheless pleased that she had pulled off a negative but in a good way. Everyone received preparation assignments from the teacher at the conclusion of class. When Manya was younger, she felt alive and like she was making a difference. She makes the decision to try and experiment with whatever arises. Now she is so afraid of things.

Manya was ready to return home. She spotted a Danish car at the gate. She was quick to recognize it. Though he could see her in the side mirror, she was going to frighten him. "I see you," he grinned. Still, she doesn't. "What brought you here?" she asks, not expecting his presents. He said, "You know your dad sent it here." "Yes," that energy wasn't present in her. In an attempt to cheer herself up, "Let's go to kathak classes," but it didn't really work. Differently not for Danish.

Manya feels a little better as it gets to her, and it will undoubtedly lift her spirits. Danish said, "Come on, I'm not going inside the institute." Numerous time she try to persuade him. He refused to be persuaded, saying, "I am good in the car." However, once she made her point, he was powerless to resist. He went after her. Due to his lack of participation in other activities, he felt a little strange. His comfort zone is where he like to be. And he want that.

When they get to Manya's guru, who isn't pleased with her, he ask, "Why didn't you tell about the accident?" She didn't think it was necessary to let them know what was going on. Danish answered, "Forget it; she was in pain." However, Manya objects to the way he opens his mouth. His statements lacked conviction. She asked him to come here since she was unsure of her decision now. He was unhappy with his statement and remarked, "Yes, her mouth was working so she could have called me." "But her hand was not working." Danish, though, was completely missing his words. It seemed as though he was making a statement. Even still, he remained silent because Manya had the ability to yell at him as well. "Okay, no problem". With a hint of serenity or angry, he continued, "I know you couldn't dance at the time, but I didn't know where you went." Danish thought he was mentally stable as well. She began to practice there after he left after her begging. With his laptop a comfort workspace.

He briefly entered the classroom after an hours. He watched everyone dance from the door. He also make a video. Upon the conclusion of class, Manya attempted to locate him, but she was unsuccessful. Once outdoors, she noticed him in the garden. He was conversing with a few females. She moved away as soon as she realized and bided her time till he finished the chat. He took a very long time. However, he acknowledges that night is falling. He approached her.

When he noticed she was seated on the floor, he asked, "Why are you here?""She got up.

She was pleased with herself, saying, "You were talking, so I thought not to disturb you."

"Don't think I'll meet girls again; I am not like those fun guys, I am nerds who study a lot, no one like my type guy." "You should definitely give it a shot," they urged as they started to head toward the parking lot. He was serious when he said, "I have tried a lot and spoiled my dignity every time, not now."

Despite his best efforts, girls never seem to find him interesting and he never seems to be the guy they are dreaming of. Over time, he developed a more sombre demeanour. He doesn't go out to clubs or watch movies. He's not a member of Generation Z. Above all, he abstains from alcohol and everything. It suits him to be silent all the time. Numerous girls were mentioned by Manya, but he believes they are the worst fit for him. Instead of looking for girls, he chooses to go with the flow, reasoning that it is best to let things happen naturally. Perhaps he will meet someone else.

A sleepy Manya woke up Sunday morning. Her father was in the kitchen today. He repeatedly tried to wake her up, but he didn't even bother to listen because she was sleeping so soundly. She was ready for no apparent reason. "Do you require assistance?" She merely requested to be generous; she doesn't want to assist in the kitchen. Without even asking, he said, "Cut the fruit." She had no idea that she would be hired. She tried, regretfully, to peel the pineapple. "You don't cut it that way," he remarked. She was chopping it vertically. With her assistance, he continued, "Go give this Danish home." She accepted the roll. And she started walking like she was jumping. When she rang the bell, nobody answered. There, she was unable to stand correctly. It's only a routine. She remained silent and attempted to listen in on Danish parent's talks, but she was unable to hear anything. Someone opens the door.

"This keema and pao dad made he said to give you," she continued, not sure how to get into the house. With a smile, the Danish's mother accepted it, saying, "Oh, thank you, Manya." There was a lull as she was unable to come up with a reason to stay. "Ah, be here, I need Danish help, I have a laptop that damage," she stammered. She ran back home, got her laptop, and went back. She was moving so quickly. Her father began to yell in Punjabi, her mother togue she never learned, but he does occasionally speak.

She came in and said, "It will take some minutes." and brought the casserole into the kitchen for them to hear. Their speech was really sluggish. The sound of the coffee maker was bothering her, so she swiftly turned it off.

"I don't know what he wants out of life; he doesn't tell us what company he works for; he is doing something illegal," his mother said, exaggerating. "He just stays up and doesn't sleep." Manya was unable to hear the correct sentence. As though she needs more time, she begins to consume cereal. She really couldn't eat the keema pao because it was meant for them, but she was hungry. She disliked the taste of cereal, though. His father was somewhat reserved and said, "I think you are overreacting." "I feel like that," she told herself. "You see, Manya, at least go somewhere and joke around. He spends the entire day in his room; he doesn't come out not even for dinner and lunch." Manya becomes a little side-tracked there. "Do I make jokes?," she told herself, "Damn, forget it, I am a joke to people." Nothing wounded her. They were speaking in such sluggish tones that she was only able to hear partial sentences. "I'm over playing the friend."

She run to Danish room with the laptop and the cereal. She was like mouse in the house. Running around, eating whatever she see, invading privacy. Perfect holiday for her. "What brings you here?," Feeling a little afraid, he asks. She tries to frighten him by saying, "You have this headphone on all day; you never know what's going to happen."

"You have my cereal, and what are you saying?, It came from friends in Dubai," he remarked, picking up the dish.

She veered off topic when she said, "I don't want it to taste bad."

"Could you please fix this laptop?," She places it on his desk and asks.

"No, I don't take free work, especially not from inexperienced actors who show up at my house without asking."

"Oh, I was wasting my time trying to help; your parents were talking about you anyway."

"What?" His expression suggests that he wants to know more, but he doesn't want to admit that he has been intrigued. How can he hide?.

"Fix my laptop first" she firmly said. Her arrangement made him silent, and he knew that if he didn't make the necessary corrections, she wouldn't say anything to him. "Alright, how would you like it fixed?" He says, opening the laptop and trying to figure out what's wrong. "Tell me the nature of the issue". Manya kept silent.

She took the laptop and stated, "There's no problem, it's actually a quiet healthy laptop; I just want to see you begging." In addition to being shocked, he momentarily experienced a pinch in his brain. He was not done thinking. She simply irritated her. "I don't want to know now," he murmured. "But I really want to tell your mother is very concerned about you and believes that you are doing something wrong at times; perhaps I'm implying that she said something unlawful at some point," she said, glad to assist. "You kept bothering me about this; I know it; she came in the middle of the night and I was sleeping on the desk; she woke me up and made me go back to sleep, but I started working from there; she got worried," he said, sounding increasingly serious. She repeats, reflecting on herself, "What a strange world you are working in, and that's the problem, and if that's not also the problem, then what is the problem?" she remarked, "She is just concerned about my health." She tries to make him laugh, saying, "Oh yeah, you look old, the dark circles," but taunting someone never works.

Yash came into the class. That was early. He was dressed entirely in formal clothing, with a perfectly ironed shirt and without a trace of a winkle. "How's your hand doing?" he inquired. "Whatever hand is better, Now it's all right," she enquired, baffled. Though the pain constantly reminds her of the accident, she occasionally forgets about it. He grinned, "I thought maybe it was still healing." "Don't worry, everything is alright now, but I'm not sure about my brain," they both said in unison, wondering what more to say. He continued to stare at her, and she returned the stare, wondering why he was acting in this way. "I've had enough staring; would you like to say anything?" Breaking the stillness, she says. "Nothing... nothing...specific," he said with a grin now.

She begins, "You have an assignment," to start the dialogue.

"Yes, I'm ready; should I show it to you?"

She instantly said, "No, I mean, you should show it on the stage." She is not interested in claiming paralogism.

❧❧❧

Manya was looking through the paper when she said, "I was thinking about the assignment all day; I have not been that prepared." She had Niti, Kartik, and Shresth with her. "Why are you so impulsive and making others too?" Shresth was still unable to decode Manya. In the garden area, they were rehearsing the phrase. From there, Yash crosses over. Manya called to Yash, "Come here," but he refused since he saw everyone else there. I.e., she did not coerce him. Kartik was always awful for Yash; he is relieved. "Why talk to this dumb," Kartik asked. Although we claim to have grown, we haven't. She was unable to respond. A disappointed nod of the head was all she gave. As she noticed Mansi with other guys, she stated, "You just concentrate on Mansi; I think you might lose the point." Kartik was a little bummed that he was unable to engage with her in the way that he desired. It's never luck that works. Manya said, "You ought to treat people with courtesy."

Manya makes an effort to be friends with everyone. She has no desire to argue with others. She brings people together, which is why she doesn't stay with just one person. She loses them all, somehow. The fact that being with everyone is a little different eluded her. Regardless of your desires, you are unable to be with everyone at once. She still makes an effort to act politely with others, which is really nice of her to try to avoid hurting them.

Niti opens Shresth's bag and pulls out a package. Shresth took it back, saying, "Hello, it's mine." She tries to take a piece of the sandwich, saying, "It's a sandwich; I'm hungry; I can take a bite at least," but once she does, the whole sandwich will be gone. With a hint of shyness, he answered, "My girlfriend made this for me." All of them go make fun of him. The football match that was going on, meanwhile, simply diverted Kartik's attention. He had the blue team's back. It was a contest between colleges. He was paying attention to them, but he wasn't really engaged. He was lost in the game and shouted, "Here they go again, now penalty."

"Observe him; he seems like a different person. He has homework, but he is showing interest in other things, I assumed he was just fond of Mansi." Manya, don't let fate to torment him.

Niti and Manya receive a sandwich from Shresth. Kartik received a small portion from Manya. She recognized it was a half-cooked sandwich of corn and spinach as soon as she took a mouthful. She gave what she had put in her mouth a brief moment of attention. She was delighted that she given a little Kartik, but she regretted her decision. No one reacted when she finished eating and turned to see why they were eating this. Everyone has received a sandwich where reacted differently, yet didn't said anything. "What is the flavour?" Kartik was intrigued. Niti responds fast, yet it's safe for everyone. "It's nice, healthy, but tastes great." Each person nodded. She stated so earnestly that no one could take offense that "In actuality, the doctor advised against eating healthily, but it was so good that I resisted it." "She is peculiar; we require a translator to comprehend her," Shresth was unable to comprehend. "Do she attend our college?," Niti wanted to know more about her. Actually, she resides in the dormitory and is pursuing an MBBS at the government institution. "She needs to study a lot; it's fairly difficult, according to what I met her about today". Shresth was glad to talk about her. As he mentioned, MBBS Manya began to imagine that she would be very smart and began comparing herself to her in an attempt to get along with her. In India medical school are so expensive that only wealthy person can afford it on the other hand, government college are best but you have to be best in studies. She definitely extra ordinary. It dawns on her that this is not possible if she has a job that is very respectable. She is unable to study very much. And even unable to administer shots. She reverted to her own self.

Taking the phone from his pocket, Shresth dialled his girlfriend's number. However, she was not answering. Manya desired to see her as well. She attempted to act as though she didn't care that she was anxiously awaiting her pick-up. Niti was primarily intrigued, but since she was standing next to Shresth and Manya was across from him, she could see the screen of his phone. Still, she managed to answer the phone. Shresth was not as excited as Manya was. "Where did you go?" He showed everyone, "I'm in college with friends; they had your sandwich and they were praising you." Since she was so near to the camera, Manya looked over her face. Manya said, "Oh, she is beautiful, wow," in a serious yet reserved manner. How does one look so attractive even at a low viewpoint? "Yes," Niti concurs as well. His partner became bashful. "Oh, very kind of you," she adds, growing bashful. Kartik looks at her as he listens to her. With the best view of both football and Shresth"s girlfriend, he was seated behind him. "How did you like Shresth, wow?" He said, not at all bashful. Shresth halted him, saying, "Stop it." Everybody chuckled. "Are you heading somewhere?, You dressed up, I thought to ask." He kept asking questions and found it difficult to stop. Shresth gave him a full-fledged stare this time. Thus, he resumed his football viewing.

"I have to study, so I'll call you later," hurriedly said his lover. Her desire was to end the call.

"Alright, you're heading somewhere," Kartik had planted the seed in Shresth's mind.

"No, I just wanted to study after coming from college," she stated earnestly.

He ended the conversation with, "Okay, see you."

Manya went back to her profound thoughts. When she discovered that Shresth's girlfriend call had not ended, she was torn between thinking she was gorgeous and feeling awkward. She took the phone up. It only displayed her room's ceiling; nothing else was visible. It attracted Shresth's attention, and he picked up the phone. Kartik approaches and looks after Manya throws a pen in his direction. He assumed something had happened when he noticed everyone's solemn expressions and thought, "What?" He sat behind the shrine once more.

His girlfriend's voice could be heard, followed by a male voice. The video lacked clarity. Everyone works so well together that not a single sound is made. "She's being held by someone," Niti said.

Everyone was swarming closer to get a better look at the guy holding her since they could clearly see each other's faces. Shresth noticed the phone call was still going on as she yelled, "Elisa." Now the drama is over. Manya told Kartik, "Elisa, what a fancy name she have." Early on, Shresth growled. Manya tried to hold off, but she was unable to stop him.

"What are doing you do?" His heart was heaving. His sight discerns. Everybody fell silent.

"Calm down, I'll explain." She was taken aback. She had not considered her mistake.

"What justification will you offer for your cheating?" He shed a tear. You could say that.

"I sincerely apologize; what should I do now?," She was also unable to explain herself.

"To be honest, I apologize; please don't call me," he sobs and hangs off.

He appears ashamed and is unwilling to speak. He stood up, grabbed his out, and headed out. Everyone remained quiet, taking time to comprehend what had just transpired. All they were doing was staring at each other. Kartik pivoted to witness his team's defeat. "Today is a losing day for everyone," Kartik said. Manya gave a small smile. Niti objected, saying, "You two are insane; you're smiling, oh my god." Kartik and Manya, though, are still giggling.

"You'll understand when it happens to you," Niti remarked. "Mom's assertion."

❧❧❧

"Do you believe we can apprehend her?," Kartik questioned Shresth, but he wasn't feeling too talkative.

Shresth was holding a can of beer, which he nearly consumed. They're lounging on the steps, a place where nobody generally goes. "You move quickly," Kartik peers out of his can. Kartik's phone rang. Manya was the one he didn't pick the call. Because, as Shresth mentioned, he was trying not to say anything. His incessant remarks and queries were getting on his nerves. However, Manya wouldn't accept his silence. It dawned on her then that they had an assignment; they had shown the teacher the skit. But now they have to do final time. As he enters the corner.

"What would you like now?," Kartik exclaims, albeit softly.

She can yell, "Don't act like you forgot; we have an assignment, and I won't receive a failing grade."

He becomes serious, "I can come, but Shresth doesn't look nice; he is quiet; he only said one line."

"What"

He didn't look like he was serious when he said, "I want beer."

"Are you both insane from drinking in college?" She was not kidding.

He summoned them, saying, "We are at the back of the building; there is a stair, right that place."

❦❦❦

Kartik jumped to his feet in horror as Manya approached. He felt as though she would strike him.

His hands went up, "I can explain."

They were having their own issue when they said, "What are you, Shresth girlfriend?" both got lost in the fight. Forget about Shresth, who in front of them.

Both of them apologies.

The only person speaking sense was Niti, who said, "Both of you are making it more complicated; we just have to go to the auditorium; we can do our assignment; it's not that complicated." Manya took a seat next to Shresth and sipped the last of the

Kartik beer.

"How come you stole mine?," They got into a fight once more.

With a straight expression, she stated, "I am also fed up; it was just half; it doesn't bother you; it's not going to bother me even."

Simply keep quiet. They off to the auditorium. "Okay let's go,", Shresth got to his feet.

"Where's my cash going? Because you drank all day, you ruined my life. This was all I had left to save myself, and it has all abruptly disappeared. Say, what you want?," With a shout, Kartik tugged Shresth's collar.

It appears that Shresth is more promising than Kartik. "Your money, it was my money; you don't know how to run a business; I am living because I am drinking; otherwise, I would be dead; I am already dead inside; let me live," Shresth said. His passionate gaze belied his temperament. When he began speaking, even Kartik was taken aback; he made no mistakes at all.

Rewatching them from backstage, Manya and Niti were shocked at how well Shresth was playing his character. "This character is made for Shresth, drunk and broken," they said. With buddies who didn't succeed, it was a skit, who are attempting to launch a company. But inexplicably, everything fell apart. Shresth's persona is on the verge of passing away.

She understood that Danish was in the audience, taking notes and keeping an eye on things.

Kartik adds, "The way you are drinking is going to kill everything in your body and soul."

"All right, that's what I'd like."

"Now is your moment; proceed," Niti shoves Manya.

"Hi, what are you doing in this place? Where are you now, I saw you?," Manya was calling and trying to find Danish.

In the parking lot, he said, "I was watching your skit."

"Yes, I did see you; were you allowed to enter?," She enquired.

Thankfully, they did, and Manya left the campus.

Before leaving, Manya intended to meet Shresth, but he had already left. As they met the teacher, they didn't meet anyone else. He goes missing. She gave up trying to find him. She should go home, she thought.

With an expression of excitement, she said, "I have a gift for you."

"What?, You possess a talent," he said without seriousness.

"While he was driving, I found your lunch box on the earth," she hurled at him.

"How did you discover it?" She is not bothered by it. To him, she didn't respond. He queries again. She uttered the words "In the dustbin" quietly. "What?" Instead, he hurls it outdoors.

She was upset and said, "I took it outside from the dustbin, and you behaving like this." Broken-hearted. "People eat in that you brought it in from dustbin; let's not talk about it further; please be quiet, I don't want to hear back story."

A minute passed in quiet. "I'm sensing this strange odour since you arrived," he sniffs. She kept silent. "What is it, speak up," he yells. She said, "You said to keep quiet, before becoming silent once more." He continued to look within for himself.

He was certain now, "It is a beer; you had a beer." In a shock.

Trying to fall asleep, she remarked, "Wow, you have a great dog nose."

"How can a college student drink beer in class?" He gave a nod. Her gaze shuts.

Turn to have an iced tea, Danish about to take U-turn, a Car was also making a U-turn to the opposite side. He indicated with a downed window as well. Typical of an Indian, he was waving his hand to stop the other vehicle. Rather, Manya flings down the window and gives him a high-five.

"Are you crazy?, Why are you dancing on the road when you have an indicator?," She chuckled. She gave him the creeps. "Are you crazy now?," she laugh because both said same words. Danish, on the other hand, found himself having to accelerate the car right away in order to avoid having to pursue them. "Why do you want to bring me into trouble?" He complained.

๛๛๛

"How come you accepted the ticket at 10:00 p.m.?," Danish was not amused by a night-time movie. For coding, he can stay up late, but not for other things.

For the past thirty minutes, she had been trying to convince him, "We will go straight home, and you can sleep." Lying on the couch was him. Not preparing to leave. Now she was sick of trying to persuade him. But he was powerless to resist his mother's arrival. He wants to appear as though he enjoys himself.

Danish went, but he was asleep much of the time. "You can watch a nice portion of the film," she urged. When Manya decides the scene is good enough to watch, she wakes him up, but she watched the entire movie. For him, he didn't know the protagonist. "Yeah, I'm watching," he said, but he had trouble falling asleep. She made the decision to have fun. He abruptly woke up and began speaking, saying, "I am trying for U.S. colleges or jobs; I don't know what I should do—study more or get a job."

"What is most essential to you, in your opinion?" She doesn't want to chat, but when he said "U.S.," she was taken aback that he had given it any thought.

"Nothing," he categorically stated.

Her suggestion was sincere: "I don't know what to do, but you should go; you have more opportunities."

The movie comes to a close. Danish seemed relieved that his ordeal is over. Now he can return home and rest comfortably. However, he noticed the game zone area, which was about to be closed. They were given one ticket to the Hammer Game, nevertheless. Each tries to strike as quickly as they can. Manya was really missing it. "Just one rubber,'" she said, gazing intently at the counter boy. She wasn't content. "Okay, we'll come back at the appropriate time next time," he adds as he pulls her outside. Messages were coming in for Manya. The sound of tingling came from her phone. It was Yash, but she remained silent. Danish knew she wasn't interested in him, so he didn't ask anything when he saw his name on the screen. He is aware of her curiosity in guys. Though it's obvious that sometimes people act differently, she is consistently critical of him. However, it may potentially cause Yash some pain because from the start, it was obvious that he was making moves and Manya was just ignoring them. Danish considered helping them, but realized it would be a waste of time when he noticed her lack of interest in her. Relationships that are forceful are the worst for everyone.

CHAPTER FOUR

Manya was waiting at the door of the classroom, looking for Shresth. He was absent from the class. He refused to answer the phone. In her seat, she sat. Her cell lit up. At last, Shresth was the one. Niti arrived and sat next to her in the interim.

"Are you coming?" inquired Manya.

He answered, "I wouldn't come today," not wanting to converse.

"Are you employed?" hoping that he won't become enraged.

"No, I just need to take a little break."

Manya gaze upon the Niti. She took out her phone and yelled, "Stop bugging people."

"I'm not pestering people; I'm just attempting to assist him," Manya become irritated.

"Did he request assistance?," Niti remained true to her assertion.

Manya fell silent and said, "No, maybe he needs help; maybe he even doesn't know he needs help." Niti stopped arguing after that. Though her remarks were harsh.

Yash was baffled as to why they were both depressed. "You meet me only when your friends are not around," he remarked, clearly troubled. "Just Shresth isn't arriving!," She uttered. When he declares, "Kartik is officially on a date," he rolls his eyes. Niti said, "Oh, he's too fast." "How come you believe I'm ignoring you? I don't have fights with Kartik, but you do". Manya doesn't believe anything that is said about her. "All right, you made your point," Yash attempted to clarify, but he was unable to counter.

"All right, good, I'll speak with Kartik," he said. He really has no intention of discussing it. Both of them simultaneously said, "Good luck," not giving a damn about him.

Manya believed that she ought to develop closer friendships. From everyone, she feels a little out of reach. She observes all of the sharing and chatting. She was considering the methods used by others. What's wrong with her that it seems too hard when it's so simple? She is overindulged. that is, Everyone experiences this.

❧❧❧

"Look, Shresth is here." He appeared less than thrilled during the intermission, although he had improved in his conversational style. It startled Manya that he didn't want to converse when he came and sat next to her. He was quiet, avoided conversation, and no one bothered him. If they converse in between classes, he can become irate and things could become messy. Manya was not paying attention in class. She was just yawning and gazing around. She thought she was doing so well till she unexpectedly encountered Mansi. And she was quite focused. Perhaps, she reasoned, what Yash had said was not true. She thought she couldn't do it because she was so adaptable when she watched her. She began listening to the teacher after having this thought, which made her feel even more drowsy.

Following the conclusion of class, Manya tries to fall asleep. With his eyes fixed on the board, Shresth remarked, "I couldn't get over the fact that it happened." "Is it something you're saying to me?," she asks. He seems really depressed. His eyes have a teary look. Manya was surprised by how much of an impact it might have on someone. She is not attached to anyone that she can relate to. When someone leaves you, or you leaves and hurts you, it hurts you so deeply emotionally that you couldn't concentrate. She was unsure of what words to offer that would be comforting. How can she console someone you don't know all that well yet? He regrets saying, "Sorry, it just came from the mouth." "Oh, no issue. Really, I am not a expert, but you are capable of overcoming any obstacle." Everything always appears to come to a standstill. "Give it some time. You're able to communicate. I promise not to share it with anyone". She speaks swiftly, but her incomprehension makes his eye bulge. She's staring at him, not sure what to do. He gives a small smile and says, "Thanks. I know we don't get along that much, but somehow I express, as you keep nagging me." "I didn't bother you," Manya emphasized, pressing her forehead. It caused her to revaluate her nagging style. "Did you converse with her?," She carried on the discussion. "I'm not really in the mood, to be honest". He was adding, "It doesn't matter to force her," as Kartik placed a hand on Shresth's shoulder from behind. He moved him aside with a shove. "My issue now surpasses yours," he remarks, alternating between them.

Manya cackled, "Don't you have manners!" at him. He gives her a glare. He lacks the energy to argue with her, though. "That's why it's hard to be friends with him," Yash said as he approached Manya holding his exotic juice. She immediately rejected it with contempt. She don't want to share food with him. And make him feel romantic about it.

"What has transpired since then?," Shresth was at ease.

"In actuality, as you may be aware...," Kartik exaggerated.

Manya laughed, "You didn't become that celebrity."

"Please be quiet; perhaps you are aware that I was with Mansi. I didn't know that she had a partner because she didn't even tell me; I just assumed that she might be able to help with schoolwork or something. She continued contacting me and always gave me preference. My freaking tiring man, I got to know today," he exclaimed. Yash got interested as well, saying, "I don't think she ever said that she likes you, and by the way, she talked to me also on message, which means she is into you." That was a bad idea to tell him. Manya tells Yash, "I think that thing applies to you also." It took a while for Yash to comprehend that he might be mistaken as well.

"Now let's just focus on him," Shresth remarked. She thought, "Don't make a scene; you are reacting like you have been in a relationship with her for months," but she expressed her feelings with glee. "Your words kill me, not comfort me," he exclaimed, going overboard.

"Even though you stated that it doesn't affect the scenario, Kartik, I don't think you get it. It doesn't make sense. Shut up being such a baby," Shresth was merely being serious.

"Okay," it doesn't imply that he had a change of heart.

At the quick movement, Manya's father stated, "I have completed the ticket; we are leaving on Friday; please pack your bag on time." He is aware of her recklessness and her propensity to act impulsively. Though he always attempts to change her, in the end, he changes his mind. It would be best to tell her again because he cannot debate with her that much. "What makes us going?" she inquired. She asked once again, "To rest a little, and also, I have work, that means be serious about it; don't make me sick." Her father's hometown of Punjab was where they were headed. She rarely goes there, but when she does, she enjoys her alone time because Punjabi village and Mumbai town have different vibes. Since she stayed put following the accident, she felt good about the strategy. She'll have a major change of heart.

Her granny visit temporarily to Mumbai. She had such loving attention from her grandmother. It was her who gave her the movie-star quality. When she had the gurguroo on, she would play her old Hindi tunes and make her dance. That's what inspired her to learn Kathak. It provides her with the grace and expressiveness she requires for acting in addition to being a dance form. Nothing will be thrown away. She wasn't old enough to recall everything, but she does recall the food and her grandmother's distinctively deep, husky voice. It's strange that she can still clearly recall her voice. As though she was in the vicinity. Gramma is the same as Punjab. However, she remembers it with joy rather than sadness.

"All right, I'll be there when it's time," she says.

He wasn't sure until he saw the outcomes, but he said, "I will see that."

Manya considered going shopping. Danish could come with him; she was going to call him. However, she saw that he appeared stressed and was working when she arrived at his residence. He didn't see her, and she didn't interrupt him. He spends a lot of time on his work. His sleep regimen wasn't the best because of this. She considered going it alone. She went to a mall and was observing a model image while standing outside a store. Believing she isn't even capable of getting there. Or this is how she'll live. She is plagued by a persistent fear of the future—the idea that even though you dream about it, you end yourself right back where you started. She has self-doubt once a week and asks herself, "If I can't prove myself, what job can I do?" She thinks of nothing. Because, in her opinion, acting and Kathak are the only things that exist.

She opted to sit in a cafe with a cold coffee instead of entering the shop. Lost in a profound emotion. Abruptly, she received a text. "How are you doing?," Danish texts her. She provided her location, but she added a five-minute timer limit this time. When she checked on Danish after ten minutes, he had arrived in the cafe.

"What brings you here? You don't have a job," she said gravely, raising suspicions about him.

"What transpired with you?, Why the severity?," He said, sipping his steaming coffee.

Calmly, she said, "I am serious; I am just saying you may have work to submit; you have your deadlines." She didn't have any coffee. She was glaring at the patrons of the cafe as they went about their business. "Why do you keep staring at people?" Act like he's not with her.

"Do you believe that the actions you are taking are appropriate for you?," She posed an inquiry. Completely ignoring his question.

"Again, I have no problem with what I am doing or what anyone else is doing, so perhaps at some point you will be able to do things that you dislike or believe you are incapable of doing; you can work here, learn a lot, and money will make people happy; I have work for others; you learn gradually, not all at once; why do you hesitate to begin? yes," He replaced the paper straw in her chill coffee as the previous one had become soft.

"You don't have to pretend like this; I don't have time or confidence," she says as she pours herself a drink.

"Remember that you came here to shop; don't ruin my mood too."

Manya visits a store. Danish takes a different route. But because he is not very active, he arrived quickly. He sat on the couch, waiting for her. It's where Manya left her phone. He grasped it. Then type in the right passcode. He didn't even pause for a moment. His finger was hovering over each app as he prepared to open her social media, but before he could do so, she got a text. That was Yash. "You have to come," he urged, opening it to reveal a family member's invitation to a party. He considered texting him back, but Manya was coming with just one bag after finishing her shopping. Danish was using her phone when she caught his attention. She bolted over.

"Why are you using my phone?" Snatched the phone right away.

Without feeling guilty, he responded, "Nothing, just checking."

"When you learn how to hack too, how can you open my phone?," She questioned, Glancing through the phone to see what he was doing. He sat himself comfortably on the sofa and remarked, "I know this old man's password, which is 1234 easy; I have seen you type passwords many times." She hastily replied, "What you were going to message, Yash," and pocketed the phone. He stands up to the outside and says, "Nothing; I saw the message; you don't reply to him a lot, and he is messaging you with no self-respect, I'm not sure who I should be worried about"

"Okay, that's not your business."

Due to traffic, they had to wait for a minute in order to cross over to the other side of the road, where the car was. He said, gravely but light-heartedly, "You should go; he looks nice, but I'm talking about his money." She rolls her eyes and replies, "You haven't met him; I don't feel attracted towards him." He remarked, "Maybe if you meet him, you will understand him better than judging him like this." "Will you please not discuss it?" He actually doesn't know anything about him, to be honest, but he felt it would be wonderful if she got out and met friends instead of spending all her time at home worrying.

Usually every person has a list of qualities that they want from their partner which almost never get complete. Maybe called it fate or your choice. In the hope for the dream partner. We forget that everyone has floss. Danish never know that what Manya want. But she love fictional boy which don't exist. Sad!!!

Choose a table by herself, Manya desires to have her table to herself. She then placed an order for coffee, which she moved into her cup to keep it warmer. A small cartoon is printed on the cup. The boy from the canteen gazed at her, perplexed as to why she had so much coffee. She accepted the masala chips as well. She then proceeded to her table. On her table, she set a phone stand. Get the chips open. Then she removed the lunchbox she had been playing with and the Bombay sandwich she had made for herself. She then put on her earphones, turned on a series on her phone, and began to eat while watching the show. Her indulgence in this was so great that she failed to even glance around. It was her time to unwind. And it's called therapy.

When Shresth noticed her, he was standing behind her, observing her phone. Attempting to determine what she was viewing, he was distracted when Manya noticed Shresth's phone reflection. She turned and said, "You scared me." Taking his coffee, he sat next to her. "You seem too engrossed in," he grinned. Both of them chuckle and say, "Yeah, I was ignoring Yash for a while; I am fed up with his public confession." He replied, "He can come here." She knows him very well now. "No, he did not like here food; he always ordered or went outside." She crammed the stand and the phone into her purse. She is trying not to appear haughty. She extended her offer of food. They both have it. "It's pleasant," he added.

"Talk to Elisa; it felt nice, even though it wasn't a good conversation," he added. She merely grinned. She is unwilling to begin the process anew. It could damage him. She counselled, "Give college more importance for a while; it will be best for you. It might bother you."

"Sure, I'm attempting".

"Should I leave?". Manya placed the invitation on the study table and showed it to her father. "You are asking for your wish very late," he remarked. When he saw the date on the invitation, he accepted. Manya asked to hear it, a rejection. She reasoned that it would be excellent if he declined to go, allowing her to claim that her father had forbidden her from going outside. However, he was so cool that he gave her permission, so now she didn't know what to do. She set the card down once more. "Are you certain?".

"Why do you want me to say no?," he asked, expecting a reasonable answer. "Simply don't go if you don't want to. What makes you want to hear from me," He yelled. With a backhanded gesture, she murmured, "Okay, okay, fine, don't get angry."

"Do you remember that we have to go tomorrow? If you are going, I will send the car. Has your bag been packed?" he said so many things. Either he know that what she heard. She hurried to her room despite paying little attention. forcing her to leave.

Manya was having a hard time making up her mind. She began to feel anxious. But then she comes to the realization that she not going marry him, which explains why she is becoming so bashful. She dressed in whatever formal attire that fit her well. She searched her closet but was unable to locate something suitable. She then donned a lengthy outfit with vivid colours, but she didn't have much for the celebration. As she exits with his father vehicle , she pays attention to her father. She wasn't sure if this was the correct place when she got there. It felt appropriate as she gazed about. The location seems opulent. She had never been anywhere like this, so she hesitated a little. She had displayed the card of invitation. She entered the lodging. Observing the guidelines that she was given. She arrived. Luckily, she had no trouble meeting Yash. He was shocked; perhaps he anticipated her absence. However, Manya felt that she ought to make this adjustment for herself. Meet individuals, give yourself time to get to know them, and then evaluate how they can fit into her life.

"Come on in, tell me how you're doing." With a hand on her waist which almost give her butterfly in her stomach, he gestured to the seated area.

She said, "I am feeling poor," after taking a quick glance around.

He teases, "I don't think that you are poor."

"This place really look exotic," she said as she sat in the circular chair with her name under the heading of social media influencer. In addition to running a business, the Yash family has opened a new hotel. To her surprise, her name appeared.

"And why is my name here?" She exclaimed, startled by what was happening, "I didn't expect it."

"I apologize. I mistakenly believed that you introduce yourself an influencer. I messaged you, and you saw that. I shouldn't have put it under your name." Manya noticed that the text had slid up while Danish was looking at her phone. "Okay," she texted him. It didn't matter; by appreciating her artwork, he was showing his kindness. Not want to come seem as naive, she remarked, "Oh, that I remember; actually, I just didn't think I would be big."

He didn't say, "I'll just come in sometime." Greeting people was his hectic task. For what he could provide for her, she wasn't upset with him. She found it very meaningful that he made sure she ate everything. When she noticed that he was issuing orders to serve, she decided not to bother him any longer. Manya glance around. She adores the place's aroma. She was eating so much that she felt hesitant to take more. She declined the waiter's offerings since she felt a little uncomfortable. But since it would be disrespectful to him, she took some kababs. She then had the idea to click the photo. It won't look good if she doesn't follow through on her decision, she decided. She doesn't have anyone to click on her photograph, even if he doesn't mention that she considered posting some photos on social media, she thought to do it. So she motioned to a waiter to halt, and he used his left hand to hold a tray as he took her picture. To be sure, she came. "What more can you do?," He concurred. Again, he clicked. Even though she was alone, it was a novel experience for her.

Suddenly Yash took phone from the waiter. Helped her for the photos which made her conscious about it. Everyone was staring at her. He invited more audience when he took Manya's hand bag so that she could give different poses. She little hesitant that someone will miss understand. She couldn't handle his sweet towards her. She turn around and saw some other influencer. Suddenly Manya overthinking mind activate and keep meddling in between that he invite her for her social media image. Or as girl who he like. She could only select negative. Her mind is against of positivity.

Yash shouted out, "Manya," in a quiet voice. He never changed, calling her the same way he did in college. Though she didn't want to meet them, she did see his relatives there. But she needs to meet somehow. She said, "Hello," to each one. His brother appears far too dissimilar from him, as do his mother, father, and older brother. They were very appreciated. "Have you had any food?" Yash's mother laughed and said, "Don't worry, people here don't eat much; you can try everything." His dad concurred as well. She stated, "Actually, I thought, I should eat much; I will look more genuine." Manya uncomfortable, but she expressed her opinion. She briefly spoke with them, and his family welcomed her with great affection. After a while, she moved aside, considering that perhaps they needed to meet other individuals as well.

She began to share photos of them online. Shresth had been sending her astonished stickers, and she was receiving responses from Kartik, who was saying, "What are you doing there." Niti being cheese. "Finally you meet the family." However, Manya put her phone away and didn't answer any messages. It was going to spark discussion, and she admire Yash. However, she harboured feelings for his brother. He was much older than she was; perhaps she mistakenly believed they were only eight years apart. She was powerless against his gaze. He has a polished businessman's appearance. She has no idea who she is. Maybe she's attracted to older guys. Both properly attired and behaved. Yash, on the other hand, was making every effort to win her over, but her thoughts were firmly embedded in his. He was right out of the movie. Her dream role in the film would be actress. His black shirt sleeves were folded, and his hair flipped back. Watches are the only accessory worn.

"What are you staring at, Manya?," Yash gave her a small head pat. When she saw him, her eyes flew out. Gazing at his brother, she wondered what statement to make. Believing she attracts men just like him. Her pathetic response was, "The interior is cool," but it was preferable to be safe than sorry. Though he didn't appear persuaded, he said nothing. Somewhere she felt bad that why she couldn't make decision. A person in front of her wanting to be close with her. He is very gentle, respectful, kind and loving but she is confuse.

She has kathak classes in the morning, so she leaves early for home. Moreover, she had a noontime flight. Or she was just tired of overthinking.

CHAPTER FIVE

Suddenly, in the middle of the night, Manya wakes up. She slept off again, assuming the incorrect position. She was viewing videos nonstop, as if it were her homework, and she was holding her phone. She remembers that her flight is at noon and that she forgot to pack her suitcase. She got to her feet on the bed and leaped to the ground. And removed the suitcases from the closet. The hardest part of her job is when she begins selecting clothes from the wardrobe. Pair the two pairs of shoes with the outfits. She was having a lot of difficulty. Then she grabbed the accoutrements. Additionally, it could be warm on the farm. Following that, she heads to the kitchen, grabs some chips, and adds some to the bag. Completed. She ran in the Kathak classes.

Manya was in the correct place, thank god. She completed all tasks on schedule. She couldn't understand, though, why her father wasn't yelling at her to hurry up. He wasn't acting the way he had in the past; she recalls that he had always become agitated. He wasn't in his room when she peered in. She considered getting ready ahead of time and preparing her suitcase, but no one was able to respond to her. After taking the bag, she arrived at Danish house. The door wasn't locked when she opened it. All of a sudden, she had energy. When she arrived, everyone had stopped talking and was simply staring at the Manya. She had noticed that everyone was seated at the dining table, chatting about something, and Danish was working on something.

"Do you have any criminal plans?" Suspecting something, she asked with a straight expression, "Why have you all become quiet?" Without saying anything, they were all just staring at her. Manya was anticipating the response. "Manya, you finished packing. Please sit down. The taxi will be here soon, and we'll go." Danish speaks with the same calmness that he always does. It only confuses her more. "I apologize for my mistake; I did not reserve your ticket, but everyone has confirmed that we are making an effort," Manya's father acknowledged his error right away. He is straightforward at all times. Manya was perplexed. Was he attempting to crack a joke? Or is he sincere?

She thought to herself, "Really, check it again; maybe it would..," as if there might be a chance. "I checked multiple times, and it's clear." Danish expressed his thoughts, but he believed he might have made a stronger argument with a different line. "We'll receive the ticket, no worries. Do you have checked?" His mother, aware of her anger, made an attempt to persuade her. "I can't name it, but I could give you my ticket. I can acquire the ticket for the other flight; then I should buy it?," he says, getting confirmation from each person. Everybody except Manya agrees.

She opens her victim card with, "I am better at home; you all go; I will stay at home, It's a depressing day." Her father attempted to remain as composed as possible, saying, "Don't start now; it's just some hours different; we will wait for you; when we arrive, then we will go home." Everyone gave Danish a stern look and said, "That's not a bad idea; you can be here; we could relax more." He chose to keep silent. Manya grabbed her bags and hauled them along. Taken a seat on the couch. Holding on to the suitcase handle. She is determined to visit that place. Her father said, "Just book it; I'm not listening to anything." Danish made a reservation.

The taxi shows up. Helping Manya load the car with her bags was a Danish's parent. He tried to reassure her, saying, "It will be nice, don't worry; we will get there and have fun like always," but she didn't appear thrilled. However, she managed to promise to refrain from starting any arguments and to enjoy the trip. Manya, though, doesn't seem to forget things readily. She couldn't get this off her mind.

INSIDE THE CAR

"Well, everyone is going to Punjab, I answers myself, stupid question," Driver posed a query and provided an answer for himself. He was cordial. "Yes, you are correct," said Danish's father.

With a hushed voice, Manya says, "I am going a little late." gazing through the window.

"Why?" The driver spoke a little too much.

"I have another flight because my father forgot to book the ticket," said in a similar tone. She looked up at him.

"She is young; it would be difficult to see how she will go," he replied in a cordial manner.

When her father said, "She's in college; she can go," everyone became silent.

AIRPORT SIDE

Everybody had checked in their stuff. After each person presented their ID, Manya just stood there with a fake pale look and folding her arms. The airline subordinate asks Manya to give her ID, saying, "And your ID."

"You thought I would be with them. Though technically I'm not with them, they neglected to bring my ticket, so I'll take another aircraft with the same airline, which will leave from the same location at a different time. I'll be here eventually," she exclaimed joyfully. The airline subordinate also questioned what she was doing, as everyone was perplexed. She didn't seem to desire a lot of information based on her expression. She murmured, lovely for Manya, "Okay, I will wait for you." Everybody goes through security checks. She gets up and bids her farewell. In reality, no one reacts to her drama. She makes use of her time by moving around the airport. She went makeup shopping and had burger. Then it was time to check her bags. "Here I am once more."

IN FLIGHT WITHOUT MANYA

No one says yes, but they appear more at ease now. They all make an effort to appear concerned for her. But it was quiet and silent. Danish responded, "Thank God Manya isn't with us," and he inserted his earbuds. Everyone scowled at him once more. In addition to working there, he enjoys music. The quietness they relish.

MANYA ALONE ON THE PLANE!

She was having some alone time as well. She considered securing a seat beside an interesting person to provide a little extra excitement to the trip. She is seated by the window. Outside, she took the picture. She was also anticipating the arrival of her seat partner. She looks at each person as if they might be her seatmates, but they all move past her. It was compact, with two rows of seats. It's a kind of plane she has never seen before. She thinks it's adorable. An elderly uncle paused at her chair. A look at the number. He moved forward because it wasn't his seat. A fun person will show up several times. The elderly uncle returned. He asks Manya, "Can you match my seat number to where it is?." When she did, she noticed the ticket. He was the fortunate seatmate. With a gesture to the next seat, she declared, "This is yours." He took a seat and opened his bag to reveal a book. begins to read. On the plane, the turbulence began. She appeared anxious. This aircraft is adorable yet scary. "I wouldn't book it ever if I knew that I get this aircraft; these small plane have a lot of turbulence," he said to Manya. "Honestly," she said, feeling unwell.

Ignoring the erroneous question, he said, "Are you going alone?"

"Yes, in actuality, my father neglected to purchase the ticket." She has prepared this numerous times. Now that taken a different trip, perhaps they have arrived. "That's bad." She is giving the speech to a fresh people this time.

Everyone comes together

Upon her landing. It appeared as though she was dishevelled; her hair was combed out. The Danish estimate that "I think she's more angry now" was accurate. However, she arrived, accepted the Danish coffee, and remained silent. She look a total mess. That is all. Danish's mom thought. Might a donut will cheer her up. *Note: Hold off on passing judgment.

Manya got a text from Yash. "Reached". She saw that message but she don't have energy to reply. In her mind she had replied him. But he never got that.

Path to Villa

There was a cab driver waiting for a long time. That defies in any way in the right moment. That's why they reserved another. There was a Punjabi driver. After gathering the four bags, he placed them in the rear. He took out his card and gave it to them, saying, "You all came so late; the agency shifted the booking to me; if anything happens, you can have my number; I can help you next time." He said, "Don't tell the agency they don't allow." He stated with a serious look, "You cannot solve everything, actually; they forgot my ticket and this man booked the turbulence plane." He was pleased to assist, saying, "This problem is actually different, but I can suggest a travel agency number."

"I think it's time for us to leave," Danish's dad saw that it was becoming late. He had concerns regarding his slumber.

WENT UP TO THE VILLAGE

Manya was asleep close to Danish when it grew dark. The fact that she was asleep made him very happy. When her mouth closes, the atmosphere shifts. However, the road did not improve. She awakened. "Aircraft turbulence, vehicle turbulence," she sniffed before nodding off again. The driver said, "Sorry, your daughter is very angry."

"I understand," her dad said.

Road is poor, but they manage to meet Manya's father neighbour, nobody lives close to Manya's father's house, although they all know him. They all arrived while they listened to the car's sound. The entire family showed up, including her niece, Rashmi Aunty, an elderly woman. In her sleep, she didn't realize that she had given Manya and her father a hug. She came quickly from her nap. In regards to his hometown, Rajeev Ji gets a little sentimental. No way could he travel that far just for work he really misses his hometown. She welcomes the Danish family.

"Why did it take all of you so long?" Rashmi Aunty added, "I was waiting from past hours; I thought you had changed your mind," Manya woke up. She intended to say the same thing. Danish puts her hand over her lips and says, "If you say anything more, I will tell you." Now he's enraged. He felt her hand bite. Shalu, Rashmi Aunty's niece was unsure about what they were doing. "Help them," Rashmi Aunty urged Shalu. Manya wanted to help to shut Danish mouth but she recall his name, she was confused. Shalu is a name for men, sounded like female. Manya takes her work very seriously. She was genuinely intrigued. However, everyone disregarded her and entered. Shalu actually responds, "It's a male name; it's just my pet name."

"Instead of saying pet name, say nick name." Manya provided further directions, but she should be appreciative that he responded. He's ignoring her now too.

Since Manya's father has been taking care of the house for a long time, it was kept tidy. He has given it to a caretaker. Everyone partakes of Rashmi Aunty's cooking. And want to sleep deeply.

Dawn, and the spirits of all were shifting. Everyone was exhausted and fast asleep. Manya's dad arrived carrying veggies. He began preparing the aloo paratha. In the kitchen, everyone is lending a hand. Manya completed the task of clearing the space. The house was characteristic of India. It has a clear space in the middle. She was going about the place. With a drop of water on her face, she raised her gaze. Without warning, it began to rain. "I cleaned with such passion," she said, continuing to stand in the pouring rain. Danish yelled, "Take those clothes; they get wet." With that, she dashed to gather the garments and entered the room. She shed only a few tears. While enjoying yogurt, pickles, and aloo paratha while sitting on the floor, it started to rain. It dawned on them that water was accumulating. The downspout was clogged. Danish tries to wipe the stick. Manya also help him. When it's cleaned. There's a strange sound as all the water moves so quickly. After changing, they move in the direction of the farm.

When Rashmi aunty shows her farm, Manya is amazed to see that it grows veggies. Despite her frequent visits to farms, she has never seen a little kitchen garden. Her personal "After all the pain, it seems fine," Danish inquires of Manya. "It's okay, I have to cook the food; it's simply vegetables that I can eat directly". Saying as she sat on the soil divide, "Too much work." She shout. "Your clothes may get soiled," he remarks, opting to remain upright. she yawned, "Better than other things."

"Yes, I do want my room back." She argue.

Danish are not particularly gregarious.

"How did the flight go?" he inquired.

"Nicely! I befriended an elderly man. I said the same things to him. I occasionally had the impression that I was in a theme park. This is life, you know—little ups and downs, turns, and mini-deaths."

"What does "mini death" mean? It didn't make logic," he realized, but his confusion increased.

"Do you believe that I'm attempting to make sense?"

"Really, no."

"Well, that turbulence"

Danish remarked, "I feel more relaxed; it was a nice trip." He encountered Manya while he was grocery shopping. Even though she was leaving for college, she continued to drop by. She didn't seem to be enjoying herself much. "Trip, we were there to have aloo paratha; we can have it here also." She was hoping to undertake some activities and travel to the highlands. She's not as excited now that she's at home. Everyone has an office, but she has time. Both of Danish's parents work for the government. Unlike their buddies, they are required to take leaves of absence for vacation, which they typically don't. Ranjeev ji is likewise a hard worker. He is concentrating more on his work. He usually feels better at work than at home.

Manya gestured to the biscuit with cream on it. Danish choose a present for her. Licked the cream. Began distributing the last of the biscuits to Danish. "You are repulsive," he remarked, returning the biscuit. It was her biscuit. This strange stuff was all observed by the store owner. He said nothing, just continued to stare at them.

In the front row of the auditorium sat Manya and Shresth. Every space was empty. The entire class was getting ready. The skit that currently exists Manya was resentful of Kartik. He has been the centre of attention and won't let anyone in practice line. He maintained Mansi in front by staying at the forefront all the time. However, they are unable to speak up because the teacher has accepted their positions. She's done what they claim, somehow. When she first started college, competition scared her. She understood now. She didn't feel resentment towards Mansi because, in her opinion, Kartik was the one who prevented her from coming forward. She thinks that perhaps the teachers will learn, and he should be able to see.

Everyone waited until they were both in order. Shresth and Manya fixed each other with stares. She fell asleep because she was so tired. "Awaken, you are currently dozing off," Shresth gently tapped her shoulder. She wasn't sound asleep. "Husband-wife role, when will this end?" she yawned. Reaching for her eyes. He took it seriously that "They are not husband and wife in the skit." She woke up and said, "You don't have to take everything seriously." As she perused the article, she was getting ready to say her line. She approached the platform. She bided by time till her turn came. Others have now begun to do their acts as well.

"It's my turn now," she declared as she moved forward to take her turn. There was a murder in this narrative about a middle-class family. In which Mansi portrays the wife, Shresth plays an interesting police officer, Kartik plays the older member of the family who was Karta, and the spoiler Manya plays the killer. , Kartik's father was killed. She acts gullible. The character was vibrant and spicy. She doesn't have a lot of lines, though. People are unable to realize that she is the true murderer because her true identity is kept a secret. She can't disagree with the teacher because she was the major character in some way.

"It's simple to cast me in doubt; my goal is to assist you and I'll keep going until the very end for this family," Manya declares. Awaiting the Kartik queue, she waited. But he had lost his seriousness. His attention was not on his line. He started to line up as soon as he noticed the Manya line. "You've killed my dad," he began to chuckle. "I know that this is not your line; I have the script," she replied gravely. That's what he did over and over. Kartik was told by Shresth to concentrate or take a nap, but he believed he could handle it. "All right," she exhaled deeply, happy that he was no longer bothering her. She leaned in and whispered innocently, "It's easy to make me suspect; I'm here to help you, and I'm going to do it until the last breath for this family." As she should, she performed flawlessly. After ten seconds of waiting for Kartik, her once-innocent countenance became irate. "What do you know? For now, I'm done." She remarked, growing irate, "You can do with everyone, but not properly with me." Kartik remained silent and did not respond defensively.

"Just say that don't want this role, don't burst on me". Kartik shouted.

"No, I am not like you steals people role."

"Uh, I steal, do you even think you are capable of any other role."

She handed Shresth the script. She then grabbed her suitcase and walked out of the theatre.

While it was entertaining to witness, everyone was unable to comprehend what had just occurred. Everyone assumed that Kartik and Manya would constantly argue over ridiculous issues. They are pals, but Manya became much more irate than normal on this particular occasion. "What you said," Mansi uttered. He still lacks a response. Taking his bag, Shresth also departed from the auditorium. Kartik then departed as well. Although Yash was watching the battle, he wasn't enjoying it. He didn't want to fight, but he also knew that Kartik would be the one to blame right quickly.

❧❧❧

"It was a bit excessive," Shresth said to Manya. She felt ashamed of herself, which is why she was behind the building. She wishes not to interact with anyone. She kept checking to make sure nobody was coming. "I was diligent about my work and did what I felt was right." She said slowly, "If I joke around, it doesn't mean I joke even when I'm working and even he comment on my skill." She still didn't want anyone to listen, even when nobody else was around.

He questioned, "Are you jealous of Mansi?" but was afraid of her. "No, I understand that she is superior to me, and I accept that, but I've reached a point where competing with her will only make me feel worse. I am content with who I am; I am working; I will make my own path; She is talented; I will receive what is rightfully mine; and despite all of my hard work, I am furious at ignorant people. I don't want feel like a fool because of someone."

"It's alright, he'll comprehend this," he attempts to comfort himself.

She was adamant, saying, "I will not fight with him; I will resolve, but right now, I don't want to talk to him." Still she is being generous.

"All right," he said, taking a back at her adult tone of voice. She's not very intelligent. At least she's making an effort to go forward. Manya didn't see the message that Kartik sent to Shresth. He gave him a call outside the university. Even if he didn't want to talk to him, he was unable to express it.

❧❧❧

"What was said by her?" He sensed that Kartik could now talk. He was silent for a long time.

"See, I'm not a pigeon that tweets to everyone; okay, got it," he stated, disinterested in engaging in petty rumours.

He remarked, "When I made you messenger."

"Alright, fine, it's not that big of a deal; people get upset and she has a reason but you were so rude just one line and you can lose relation with people still she'll work it out; don't worry, she expresses her feelings." Everything is nicely conveyed by Shresth.

"Did she not say anything further?"

"What's desirable to hear." Everything she said, he didn't feel concerned that what he was doing truly Shresth doesn't know what he say? "She wants to kill you," What he was attempting to communicate perplexed Shresth a little. Kartik remained silent, offering no words. Aware of his mistake, he continued, "Don't you think she likes me."

"Hell no," Shresth said with a straight face. At that moment he can bet his life but he was sure. Nothing can be hidden from his eyes.

"You liked Mansi; what's that? I never saw her like that; she doesn't feel anything." He went on, "If it was that, you could see it in her expression, but she was angry." Even he got because of his rude remarks. She is competent, but she isn't sincere about it. He went a bit farther, but he began to picture the situation that he felt in the auditorium when Manya moved closer and delivered the phrases, "I felt something like I couldn't tell, I didn't feel like for Mansi, I am asking you because she talks to you, or you like her."

He blurted, "I really would like to die."

"What do you mean?" Kartik wasn't on board.

"Yash likes her because, as far as I know, she met his family, but she is not interested in anyone," the man said, adding, "I mean, as a friend, she is fine, but... I cannot imagine; she is complicated." In actuality, Kartik was quite certain, "I am not Yash." Shresth didn't understand how he could feel love in that circumstance. It's obvious to all that she will bring him down. He thought, it would have been better that if she punch him. His all doubts would have been cleared. However for him, love is a fool, and perhaps those who believe it are also fools.

"Have a good weekend?" After a great deal of persistence, Manya gave in to Yash. He was aware of her unhappy disposition. He noticed that she was worn out on stage. Anyone can see that she is having difficulty at the theatre, and although she wants to help Kartik, he merely irritates her more. "Please can I drop you off at home," he asked. Her refusal had little to do with shyness. However, she was craving pani puri. She told him, "I want to eat," in a very lofty tone. She declines because she fears that her demands may be excessive. For her, Pani Puri serves as a stress reliever. When the spice hit, it woke you up.

She doesn't feel anything since she knows that if they go closer, only Yash would suffer harm. Because she knew that they can't get in a relationship right now. But she was just dreaming to be eating pani puri in this scenario.

She forced a smile, saying, "Not that exciting, but it was fine."

"Why become upset in class?" he questioned.

"Whoa, that was really dumb. It's alright now; unforeseen events do occur."

"Would you like to have lunch?" he asked, a little hesitantly.

"Oh, it's okay, I had guests over at my house," no one is coming.

Inside the car, there was stillness. Though Yash's worried expression gives her a food-related feeling in her stomach. She had some guilt. He had unrealistic expectations. She was about to leave as she arrived home.

She was gripping the door handle when she said, "Yash, can I say something to you honestly?"

He begs, "Yes, please," hoping for something pleasant. He get closer to shut the door.

"You invite me to parties and treat me nicely, so I know you like me and are wonderful, but I don't feel anything and don't think I'm ready. People always tell me that I'm a vulnerable girl." She was so embarrassed to add, "I am very self-aware, so I am telling you now so that you would get hurt." She had a blank, scared face.

He scrambled, "Me!, who said.. that I like you.. maybe you have some confusion."

"Oh my god, you detest me."

"No"

Both of them chuckle awkwardly and say, "Okay, cool, that's the best; I am such a fool."

He made a dramatic about-face in his statement. Manya was also perplexed. But he's retracting his statement now that he knows he never meant it seriously. She felt enraged. There, she appeared foolish. Grabbing the bag, she raced to her apartment.

· 59 ·

CHAPTER SEVEN

Danish was sprinting across the ground as he ran. They're sprinting as well. It seemed sensible to start the day with a nutritious meal. Taking out his headphones, he paused and selected a different music. Looking over his shoulder, he saw Manya was running in his direction as well. Since he was now further away from her, he began to run. Her running was terrible. She lacks endurance, therefore she was unable to catch up. Observing that the elderly were doing better than her, she attempted to run more quickly.

"How do you spend your mornings? How can this possible you usually sleep at this time," she gasped. She moved to catch up with him. He slow down for her. He was fine up until this point. "I thought to try jogging; it's felt great, but I know I will not continue it," he said. "Yes, it's pretty challenging," she admitted, given up and unable to go on. "What drew you here?" He halted and enquired as well. "I was going and I just copied you," she exclaimed as she hurried to the apartment. And Danish was done for the day.

"How did you spend yesterday?" He asks directly, "You were talking to someone; I saw you." They were mask-putting and cleansing their faces. "Yash was the one who insisted on dropping; I want to eat but I can't," she said, trying to cover up more queries. He knew she had more, so he said, "That's it, nothing more."

She looked embarrassed as she said, "Okay, okay, I was being considered, so I said that I don't like you, and he said that who said that I like you." She couldn't convey her feeling in a right way. Still she was be exasperated. But he let out a big laugh. She was upset and wants to express her feelings, but she doesn't want to reveal it just yet.

He mocked, "You think that you can assume things."

She underlines the word reject. "No, he doesn't want to look like I reject him, but actually, it's true that he likes me," she says. Very sure about it. She added. "But he backs off because I said first and he fool me."

"You think this, and I know it's true, but you look foolish right now."

"Yes, that is true."

❧❧❧

"Did you experience another mishap?, You don't reply," Shresth said to Manya as they arrived at the gate. She didn't answer when he tried to phone her. She fell asleep after running, and her body wasn't feeling well. She seemed worn out and confused. Her outfit upon returning from college was casual. She was not moving in her typical gait. Her steps were light and slow. Still she don't forget to post on her social media. She said, "Don't judge me, okay? I tried running today."

"Alright, I understand, but you walk like duck," he didn't understood.

To enjoy kullad chai, they selected a seat. Manya could even take a brief nap. They relish the tranquillity and the tea. "Why do you speak in such manner?" Even though it was an unknown voice, it seemed familiar. Glancing around, they believe they might spot someone. Manya said, "Look there," pointing to someone. It was Niti; she was conversing with someone behind the tree. It was as if she was arguing with someone on the phone rather than conversing. They are unaware of her words. It was confirmed that Niti was related to someone stranger. They attempt to interpret her words.

Manya concur with the Shresth hypothesis as well. "She never tells," Manya worries about other things. He said, "Maybe she doesn't want to tell you," it hurt Manya. Noting that she never told anyone and, oddly enough, that no one had ever questioned her. From behind, they listen to her. They reasoned that she would stop talking if they bothered her. She burst into tears. Shresth wanted to say to Manya about how intense it was becoming that they should help her, but Manya declined. She disagrees, saying, "Don't disturb her; she could get angry." When Niti approached them, she could see they were conversing quietly, but she was still able to hear them. "Alright, Niti stop, why are you crying now, do you want to talk" she stumbled murmured.

"Who was the caller?" Manya was curious to hear what she had to say. Stop her, Shresth, from getting too intimate. She then fell silent and let it some time to sink in. Manya said, "You have a boyfriend," she ask directly. Couldn't handle her long tight lipped.

"She don't want to talk about it," Shresth said, staring at her. "Excuse me," she said, hushed once again. "Indeed, it is true. I'm having a little trouble since he doesn't trust me at all; he wants to know everything about me. I understand that his goods irritate me, but sometimes I get upset too," Niti said melancholic. "So why do you hang around with him?" Manya spoke directly to the point. Shresth no longer believes in her. "So, politely discuss the reasons behind your arguments; it wasn't good." He apologizes,

"Sorry that we listen to your conservation." Manya did as well. "Speak to him in person rather than over the phone, figure out a solution to your problem, or take a break and consider something you both agree upon," Manya advised. Surprising herself, Shresth felt she finally said something sane.

Niti turns her head down and says, "No, he's not bad; actually, sometimes I behave stupidly." She was trying to make a point that they could both see. "You have to discuss it maturely; I'm not saying you two are bad; I'm just saying the conversation you were having wasn't going to help," said Manya.

"He is in Delhi for some work; he is not here."

He responded, "So let him come, then talk to him."

With tears in her eyes, Niti says, "Actually, he said to come with him to Delhi, but I have college; you know, I cannot leave it from here; he is not talking with me just get angry with anything

I say." Neither of them knows what to say. She appears delicate and dejected.

"It's okay; don't rush; you're anxious; you have your college education; you shouldn't sacrifice your career; don't feel so bad when he approaches you talk him politely," Manya calmly remarked.

"Indeed, you are correct." She sipped her tea and stated, "I want relief in my life; I am panicking over small things." The two of these words soothed her. Her smile reappeared. Even though she doesn't solve her problem. Still she want to calm right there.

Shresth moved out of the way to let Manya attend the class. "Why are you leaving?" She tries to get in his way. "You disturb me in class," he snapped, offering an expedient explanation. And took off. She didn't understand why he did that. Kartik walked over to her; she could tell he was eager to chat. She gave him no resistance. He went to sit next to her after she did. "I apologize for my excessive reaction." She starts by saying, "Go wherever you want now that you are free." "No, I should be sorry; I disturbed your work, I was mean to you," he said, grinning, leaving Manya perplexed as to why he was feeling so joyous at the moment. She remained silent and accepted the apologies, just as he did. She wants to stop talking now. It will be more tranquil to remain silent than to argue over pointless issues.

She was focused on the lesson when she saw Kartik was looking directly at her. He turns his face when she gives him the side-eye. "Do you believe that I am ugly?, quit grinning," she cautioned him.

He remarked, "This is how a fight starts."

"I didn't even say anything." She stopped talking too.

She felt that was appropriate because she easily gets heated. Attempt to maintain her composure. Focusing on taking notes. Kartik was not taking anything seriously; he was preoccupied with something else.

Manya became even more suspicious when she noticed that Shresth was observing them in the interim. He turned around after taking a peek. He turned back once Manya and Shresth exchanged glances. "What he is doing," she told herself. "Who, what?" he heard her. She realized that neither of them would be able to assist her, so she chose not to tell him. Class was going to end soon.

"You must decide on a public space. Go there in a group, then each person chooses a person on their own; don't bother them. Sketch them like a character. Describe their look, expression, and face. Take note of potential career paths for them. Instead of adhering to stereotypes, you should watch how people develop. Even if can you only create an existing character, you succeeded. Form a group of your own, and then, using the characters you have created, compose a tale about them and have them perform it for me. Next, which will also have an impact on your project, you must get ready for the act and make intelligent team selections." The teacher assigned them this assignment, which was challenging, but Manya appears extremely happy. "You will learn observation on that basis and making stories; otherwise, you can make stories here sitting but going out observing makes characters alive," he said. She wishes to carry out this action.

❧❧❧

The team consisted of Manya, Kartik, Niti, and Shresth. Yash wanted to come, but he refrained from showing up in order to avoid appearing desperate. Following the humiliation, he barely moved. He's hesitant to talk even if he wants to. He continued to deny it when Niti questioned him. Wind up missing the chance.

They make the decision to visit the train station. Going to a railway station doesn't seem like a good idea because Mumbai's trains are always packed. They gather together and focus at a single location. They become disoriented as they swarm. The question of whether we can leave this location and move somewhere else is up for dispute. However, Shresth's concept that he wanted something near the train station was what started it. His writing abilities are strong. And everyone else can assist in creating the story's bridge. They waited until some space between them and the crowd. They sat down soon so they could write more comfortably.

Manya spotted a woman with un-styled hair who was wearing a saree. She applied no makeup. With a downward gaze. Watching a train arrive. She sat quietly by herself. She made an attempt to predict her next move. She left off the sindoor and mangalsutra since she didn't think she was married, but she might be. She found it difficult to comprehend. She was journaling everything she was thinking about herself. She began drawing her on the bench of the train station, her saree billowing in the breeze, her tense expression, and a tiny purse tucked within. They were all split off, focusing on their respective topics. The throng began to arrive out of nowhere. Everybody is leaving their location and heading to the railway station. Upon noticing the women standing, women hurried to her department. She was lost in the crowd for Manya.

At a nearby cafe, they enjoyed tea and bread & butter while sitting together. The sketch was written by Shresth. He came up with the story's theme, and everyone else assisted him when he ran into difficulties. They almost finished the story, but they have to provide the teacher with the script first.

Last day of the play

Danish put a lot of work into their skit, so Manya phoned to watch it. Despite his lack of time, he made an effort to support her and made it there. Manya's hair was not sitting, and she was dressed in a saree similar to the one the woman was wearing. She attempted to emulate her. But donning a saree is a hardship for her. Niti did her saree-fitting. Kartik has on a modest shirt and pants outfit. Shresth and Niti were dressed casually as well. "Your attire complements ours," Shresth remarked, glancing at Manya.

"She drew a portrait of the character," Niti remarked.

"I'm terrified of sarees." She set down because of her saree and remarked, "I have never worn the saree."

They were the next group in line for the skit, so Kartik called them together, "Let's go next, our turn." The set wasn't heavily invested in. Simply positioned a bench in the middle.

Scene 1: Kartik and Niti.

On the dining table, they were eating lunch.

"We are having our last meal together," Niti remarked as he placed chapati on his plate. He pulled out. "But I am not so hungry now," he replies, pushing the platter to one side. She stopped eating and stated, "You used to like food; when I prepare for you to at least finish it." "I used to enjoy food, but not anymore," he remarks while inhaling deeply. She continued, her expression both sorrowful and irate, "You have changed a lot; you used to like me and food, and now you hate both." She couldn't even look into his eyes.

With confidence in his choice, he declared, "I don't hate you; we have different lives; I don't think we should be together anymore; it just makes things worse." She looks up hopeful, "You have made the final decision on your own; you don't even want to try," she says. His words were focused and beseeched: "Better you start what you want to do; please don't hurt yourself and me; this is not going anywhere; I have my career and cannot give time and love."

With a hint of crankiness, she said, "I hope that whatever we take, we won't regret it."

"You'll be glad you did; remember when we were content. Please tell me." He looked directly into her eyes and spoke directly to her. There was nothing she could look at. She was trying to think, but she was stuck. Quiet is she.

He handed her a box containing her belongings and stated, "You know the answer, just that you won't want to accept it." He then left to get his luggage. Her head lowered, she said, "You should go; traffic can get worse." It doesn't even make sense to them, so they don't even embrace. They have no desire to take the lead. After gathering his belongings, he headed out.

"Are you okay?" He said, "I know I can't relieve you like I used to, but you can still call me if things weren't good."

"You can reach me as well; I'm fine," she remarked.

Scene 2: Kartik and Manya

Manya was waiting for the train on the bench. She feels uncomfortable because of the heat. She got up and went to buy herself a bottle of water. She took a big gulp of the water. When Kartik arrived, Manya was frantically waving her clothing in front of her face due to the heat. He observed both sides but was unable to locate a seat.

"May I take a seat here?" he inquired. He suspected she could find it awkward.

"Alright," she said without glancing at him. That gave him a peculiar feeling, but he didn't want to bother it.

She kept returning her gaze to her phone. She'd put it to no use. It occurred to him that perhaps she was awaiting a call or a message. It was the train horn. It would arrive. He examined the seat once more. Taking her ticket, Manya just stared at it.

"You need any assistance," he inquired. She kept silent. She whispered softly, "I have H seat; where it will stop, I don't understand," she was staring up at board. He responded nonchalantly, "Oh, that's the same for me; you just follow." Without ado. Her seat was in the next compartment, as he could see when he took the ticket.

Scene 3

While reading a book, Kartik was interrupted by Manya, who placed her bag on the bench across from him. She sat down in her seat and added, "Actually, there was family, so they changed seats with me." He chuckles, "Oh, family always switches seats," but she just smiles.

She sipped water once more. Her water supply ran out. He was aware, but remained silent. She was going through her bag. She was carrying a tiny bag, which made it odd. He was staring at her, unable to ask any of the many questions but he wanted to.

"Did you say anything?" As she saw him staring at her, she came to this realization. At last, he said, "No, really, I thought you needed more water." She put her luggage down and said, "I just want to take my medicine; it's not important; I will buy it when the train stops." He heard the medication. He handed him his water in a hurry.

She responded, "It's okay, I can have it in a few hours."

"This is fresh water don't worry; I didn't drink it. No big deal," he argued.

He repeatedly stated that she was powerless to resist. "Stop," he said, reaching for a sip. He didn't let her drink. "You ought to have something before the drink," he replied, pulling a tiffin out of his suitcase and giving it to her. She didn't know and didn't feel like taking it. She was starving, though. She still rejects it. He pushed her once more. She accepted the lone pickle and aloo paratha. Roll it up and dig in. He also gave her medication.

"Why don't you have any luggage?" he asked.

"I am actually going home; it was a last-minute plan. I already have everything I need, so I don't need anything more." She brightens as she speaks of her mother, saying, "I am excited to see my mom after three years." He grinned too, saying, "Wow, it would be great, reunion." He wonder why she didn't meet for three years. He gazed at her without any shame. She not sure why he was unable to stop glancing at her. "And you?" she responds. He seemed cheerful as he said, "I'm not going home; I'm going to work, but I love it; I think I will feel at home there." After several hours, he saw that she appeared content and relieved. She was looking out, her hair billowing.

Train comes to a standstill. "Look at this pineapple I had as a kid, seasoned with salt and chili," he remarked, turning to face the vendor. "Would you like some?" She got up in her slipper and requested. She moved fast to get where he was going to halt him. But even though she now appears joyful, he didn't stop her. Thus, he gave her permission. Because he was fear that might she can fall. She decided to purchase some berries after seeing some. She appeared surprised when she returned.

"Where did you go? I tried to get in touch with you," Shresth said.

When she arrived, her smile vanished. Kartik seemed anxious about the situation.

Shresth grinned but sounded mocking as he said, "She is my wife; she didn't tell me she was going to Mumbai." He put his hand on her shoulder. "That's all I want to do is go home," she stated, shutting her eyes. "How are you going home by yourself? It's you who's expecting," he said. Kartik look at her. She was pregnant, but he was unaware of it. Nonetheless, there was still melancholy in the way he loved her. She inhaled deeply. The fact that they were conversing in front of him made her appear ashamed.

"Well done," he remarked.

She handed over the berries and pineapple and said, "Thank you."

Shresth laughs, "Not for me," since he doesn't receive any.

She repeated this, just as she had when Kartik first met her, "He gave me water and food; I am thankfully of him." She was no longer the person he liked. Couldn't stand for her. He desired her happiness. Shresth shakes hands with him, "Oh, really, then I am also thankful for you." Kartik was unable to speak. The train was supposed to restart as soon as the siren went off. Shresth got up and grab her hand, saying, "Let's head back home." She looks at her hands, Kartik. He clung to her.

"Where?, My mom doesn't have seen me from years I want to go."

"You cannot to leave at this time," he said. There, Kartik is just silent.

"The day never..." she said, growing silent.

Placing his hand on her shoulder, he added, "I will take you promise; now that the car is waiting outside the station, let's go." Kartik took a post.

"Bye" he uttered.

He wants to say more. "Are you okay?, don't struggle alone ask for help," he inquired.

"Yeah, I'm okay," she replied. She smiled but she wasn't happy.

END

Everyone applauds them and gets to their feet. Others come, and they quickly made the changes. Their performance was satisfactory. They proceeded to the dressing area. Talking about the things they could and could not have done. Everybody has unique perspectives.

This is where the drama ends. "You're still staring at me, but why?" From the act, Manya noticed that Kartik was staring at her. She giggles. She thought it was so real, somewhere. Confusion aside, perhaps he is that good. He remained silent and moved away while she changed. She pivoted to gaze at him, curious about his situation. "Why is he acting in this way?" she used to argue constantly. He's silent all of a sudden. But she didn't bother.

"Is anybody present?" With haste. Manya went outdoors and left her luggage. She looked around to make sure no one was listening. There's nobody there, so she peeps out the door to check. Kartik heard her voice and said, "Hey, you want any help?" and arrived. She shut the door right away. She gave a slight shudder. "Why are you in this place?, This is only for women," she yelled. Even knowing that, he couldn't help but wonder if she needed any assistance. Though he didn't ask, he was aware that she required a bag. Knowing her suitcase was beneficial for her, he continued, "I am leaving the bag outside your door and I am leaving too; don't worry."

She glanced about for a while before going outside. She noticed Kartik waiting for her outside, but no one else was there. She was surprised when he reappeared out of nowhere. Taking a deep breath, she continued, "Stop haunting like a ghost." All he did was laugh it off. She still thinks it's cute that he waited for her outside without showing her how he felt. She love the pretend game. And get her an energy drink. He didn't like to communicate things with her, so she was apprehensive, but the shift in his personality was both beneficial and strange.

They strolled towards the entrance. "What are you up to these days?" She made no direct inquiries. But why he assumed she was requesting an update on her daily life was beyond him. All are attempting to secure any kind of work or internship. He informed her of every recent predicament he had encountered in the field. They sat and talked for a while about their jobs and daily lives. They lose track of their class since they are immersed in it so much.

He was so devastated by the unexpected transfer to Mansi that he initially believed she would be the ideal spouse for him. Although their chemistry didn't work at all, she seems like fun. They share comparable interests and come from the same stream, but their discussions couldn't be more different. With slow motion, they slid apart. Though not for each other, he didn't think poorly of her.

❧❧❧

"Have you attended college?" Danish was asked by Manya, "I didn't see you." He arrived late to lunch. "Yes, I did come, I watched, and it was good. I didn't tell you because I had already left after a call." "Although I didn't see you, it's good that you watched it," she remarked, relieved that things had finally worked out. "I now know why you wanted to pursue this line of work," he said. "I'm not sure, but that seems correct to me. Fun, in my opinion. I hope to accomplish this as well as I can," she prayed. He pulled out his phone and searched for the post he had seen. "Oh, I saw an audition on this post for some advertisement; try it," he said. He handed her the phone after setting it down on the table. She believes that in order to hone her abilities, "I should finish my graduation first, then I should audition." He took back his phone and said, "You can try; it's not mandatory to do that."

"OK, I'll have a look at it."

CHAPTER EIGHT

Manya spent most of her time these days hanging out with Shresth. They have ample room. Shresth speaks infrequently, although Manya speaks frequently. Sometimes they sit in silence and appreciate the peace of it by being silent. They both attempted to concentrate on their work. Reading and writing scripts are two things Shresth is learning to do. He comes to the realization that he is not as horrible as he had believed. And made the decision to attempt to test out for the commercial. Manya went down to attempt to sleep because she was tired. A whispering voice caught her attention. She cast a glance around, thinking that perhaps someone would be present. "Is Niti present?" She queries Shresth. "Stop interfering in other people's affairs," he said. She said nothing.

Just as Manya and Shresth heard Niti had been arguing over the phone a few days before, Shresth suddenly stood up. She wasn't fighting today. Talking politely, only talking about something. She said, grinning the entire time, "I need to buy some clothes, but I will come after a few days." She looked around and noticed Shresth. Manya took part also. They thought that she will be arriving. They move on.

"You're bothering her now that I told you she was somewhere," Manya said to begin their dispute.

"I was just wondering, What is she doing there?, I'm not doing anything." He's unable to offer an explanation.

"What do you mean? Simply accept it," she said.

"Alright, alright, I thought what might she be up to," he concedes, acknowledging reality.

She returned. Her smile betrayed her happiness. Manya remarked, "You look like you got some film." "I will someday," Niti said as she took a seat. She was also browsing a shopping website. Choosing her own wardrobe, Manya began to assist voluntarily. Without even asking. In fact, she was confusing her more. "Alright, I'll choose on my own," Niti struck her. As Manya rubbed her hand, she murmured, "You can use your mouth say something." While he was using his laptop, Shresth questioned, "Why are you so happy?"

"In a few days, I'm heading to Delhi," she stated, her buying yet unfinished.

He remarked, "But you wanted to concentrate on studying."

"I'll be there for just one week, and I'll give my medical," Niti stated.

Manya says, "What medical problem are you going to take?" She has a tote full of justifications. "I'm considering it," she remarked nonchalantly. "Don't you think you could end up in trouble for it?" Shresth took offense at that. "They won't understand, and I'm able to take a break from my studies." "You're stopping her, but why?" Manya added, "She wants to meet her boyfriend." she gets upset.

"Why do you think she's right in this?, Teachers will question about you not even attending courses, so I'm not saying you shouldn't enjoy yourself, but there should be a balance," Shresth added. "Calm down, my only concern is living," she said as she got up to leave for the hostel.

She was gone, and Shresth was shocked to find that she had once been a sensible person. All of a sudden, he is reconsidering. Manya was at ease. She didn't give this much thought. "How come you said nothing to her at all?" He felt resentful of her. "I argue that she has made up her mind about what she wants and won't understand our advice. She needs no advise, so I can't make her do anything. This existence is so damned telling." She remarked, "Maybe it's not so horrible that what you think can work out well." Somewhere in there, Shresth concedes that he shouldn't coerce others. He has been hurt once he don't his friends also get broken. He burst out laughing, saying, "Manya, you don't know your problem, but you know everyone else's."

"What do you mean?" she asked, slapping him with a pen.

Shresth continued to tease her. He was being ignored by her. Abruptly, she noticed that Yash was approaching them from a distance. She whispers, covering her face, "I think he is coming here." Every time she saw him these days, she became naive. He answered indifferently, "He's not a monster; he just likes you." She is concerned, though. She says, wanting to run away in shame, "I told him that I don't like him, but he refuses to say that he like me." Shresth laughed heartily. It was not what he expected from her.

Once more, he teases, "You're bad, he is so sweet."

"I prefer spicy over sweet," she declared.

"Spicy is tasty, but it aches the most."

"Sweet and slowly damage you with diabetes"

"I suppose you receive nothing."

When Yash arrived, he gave Manya a paper right away. Even though he remained silent, he wasn't upset with her. His eyes are gentle, as she saw in his eye. He was still bashful. She doesn't like him, so even if he could have said what he wanted, it wouldn't make sense in his opinion. "Is this a file for divorce?" Shresth grinned. He was met with a simultaneous look from Manya and Yash. He states firmly, "This paper does not belong to me; you left the paper it in class, so the teacher told me to give this paper to you." Shresth was pleased with himself, saying, "Yes, I did count the three times you said paper."

"Please ignore him," she begged.

With an irritated expression, he says, "I really am trying very hard."

Manya was awaiting her audition turn. Although she didn't go try out for herself, she did observe her friends going. Many of the folks there appeared capable of succeeding. A few felt uneasy as she read them. She didn't seem all that sure about it. One by one, she were assuming the name. Some may have screwed up because they came out so tragically. Trying to read faces, that's what she was doing. She eventually understands that she must put her own needs ahead of those of others, what others do: She retreats to a corner and attempts to perform her lines. Since it was an advertisement, it wasn't all that much. She didn't yell since she waited for so long.

She's back at her seat now. She noticed that Danish had arrived in her search. She waved as she lifted her hand. There she was. He arrived there swiftly. "What brought you here?" She felt humiliated. It wasn't a major issue. "I'm not going to take any action here," he declared. As soon as he understood that it was a location where the attendees might stay. He considered walking out of there. "I should have waited outside," he said. "You can go if you want to go home." A moment later, someone called her name. Despite her nervousness, she hurried to go there because they are running out of time. She wishes to avoid wasting.

She feared that by now they would be worn out. She did well, though. Nor was she depressed. There was a surge of contemplation on her actions. Danish inquired about the audition as she got to the car. "I don't know; I did do everything they asked, and they didn't respond to me." She was still analysing what she had done inside when she said, "I think it was fine." She don't want to overthink so she declared. They enjoyed some sweet and sour syrup and crushed ice to help them relax.

⌘

Manya was in the rickshaw and says, "Hello, say fast; I cannot hear you; there is so much traffic." There was excessive speeding on the road. While on the phone, Kartik was attempting to locate the cafe where her friends were waiting for her. But she was unable to hear him. He said, "Come to the cafe where we went last time." She responded inadvertently. Agreed with him.

"Do you understand or I should message you?" He was unsure. "I understand what you said". He couldn't figure out what she responded. He waited for her.

Since she missed the morning class, she believed that she ought to attend the other class. Nevertheless, she paid attention to him and decided that perhaps there would be any employment, so she went to the location. She went in, looked around, and was unable to locate him. A vintage Parsi cafe was there. The antique vibe of the cafe is fantastic, even if the space was packed. She adores it because of the bread's aroma. The sound of cutlery and conversation from various persons can be heard. Although there may be noise here, it's part of the atmosphere. Her search was on. She was observing what other people were consuming as well. Accelerating her appetite.

She didn't realize Kartik was right behind her until he grabbed her wrist and said, "Hey." The fact that she has at last met someone brings her relief. She searched for others, but there was nobody in sight. "You can release my hand," she remarked abruptly. She went to the seats with him. "Where's everybody," she enquired. She believes nobody will show up. The fact that he was not responding made sense to her. "Look, I'm not able to assist you for Mansi," she abruptly remarked. He was astounded by her remark and remarked, "I'm not asking for help." Immediately, the waiter arrived to take the order. Ordered were two omelettes. They were awkwardly staring at each other, not knowing what to do with themselves here. Just Kartik is aware.

"Who will cover the cost?" yet another impromptu inquiry.

He remarked, "I assumed you were going to inquire as to why we were here."

When the food arrived, she said, "My next question is going to be this," and she began to eat. She gives him the spoon. She ate quickly so she could make it to the next lesson on time. "You didn't answer anything; I am skipping the class for your sake; the reason should be good," she remarked. He went after her. He attempted an apology, saying, "I thought we always fight; sometimes we should talk." She ceased eating as she mentioned. Because of this, she was taken aback when he called her right away. "We completed the job together, so I'm not upset with you right now. Why are you upset?" She resumed eating, assuming he would decide that. "Nothing really special but I wanted things to be more relax".

"You should think after the classes"

Yet Manya didn't want to spoil the mood. She pushed herself to have a nice conversation with him. As soon as the bill arrived, she jumped to pay. Still, he said, "You don't have to pay; I called you." She said, "It's okay, I paid because I eat more than you," as she prepared to leave for college.

They stroll along the road. Kartik made a lot of effort to engage in dialogue and speak up. She struck up a discussion, saying, "What you going to do is act; you always get the lead role; you might get a lot of gigs." He starts by considering himself. He says thoughtfully, "I don't have any priority at the end of college; I could find my focus, direction, or acting." He occasionally attempts acting and direction as well, but everyone recommends him for the role. And he performed that task admirably. Kartik merely follows the crowd; he doesn't take anything seriously. He has faith that fate will lead him to the ideal location. He was aware that he was useless in other professions. Thus, he simply supports his family by doing that. All he does is enjoy life and wait for his fate. She smirks and says, "Oh nice, I wish that at the end of college I could really understand you."

"I wish we stay together"

It was a red on the road, but Manya was going to cross it. It was green for a moment, and then it changed red, confusing her. She was unaware that the timer had run out. The bike goes by her as she strolls along the street. Pulling her hand, Kartik asked, "Are you okay?" She was so startled that she was unable to process what had occurred. She missed what he was trying to say because it was spoken so quickly. It brings up memories of the mishap. It stuck in her memory, for some reason, even now. Recognize that she might be irresponsible.

He often asks, "Are you alright?" She regained consciousness. She took a long breath and said, "Oh, it's fine; actually, I didn't understand what I was doing."

He holds her hand as he crosses the street and adds, "You can be late; there is no rush; we will reach the class." They stay together the entire way to college. "Why do you always hold my hand?" She enquired. He refused to let go of her hand and remarked, "Because I don't want to go to jail for your murder, like you behave on the road." Still doesn't convinced, "Alright, alright, but now it's weird," she pulls her hand in response. Manya notices something is off when she glances at Kartik. "Why was he acting so kindly toward her all of a sudden?" She experiences stomach butterflies as a result. Manya was confused why she get some butterfly moment. Didn't getting what is real and fake. "Am I bad person". She ask herself.

Once they get to college, she meets Yash, and that's when the awful things start to happen. Because of Kartik, she assumed he would ignore her, but he approached her and began to follow her. While strolling together, the three did not exchange words. After a hello. Just quiet when Manya say hey. They were ignoring each other when she turned to face them.

She made fun of them both, saying, "I never saw two kids in college fight for a silly thing."

Kartik says, "I will solve the issue immediately," and he headed for a hug. And Yash refused to get love.

"You just say things you don't mean to say," Yash said, showing no interest at all. Manya pushed Kartik down, placed her earpiece down, and turned to leave. "Stop, alright, we're going to act like classmates, at the very least," Yash said. Manya turn to observe their polite but meaningless handshake. "I hope your relationship succeeds," she remarked as she turned to go. They both stroll with her once more. "Do you require a handshake from me?" She said, taking out the earphone and enquiring. They gave a nod. "Where were you with my friend Kartik?" Yash asked, his eyes wide. "We have omelette pav and he bluffed me," she stated without even glancing at them. "Oh, that's nice. Why did he lie to you about the meaning of that?" He was inquisitive. "It's not what you think; we fight all the time, and I wanted to strengthen our friendship," he says. They appear to be insulting one another rather than really making an effort to speak. "What strength?, are you going for a war".

"I never get your way with you.

"Why do I want to settle with you?"

They get into an argument. As all of this is going on, Manya leaves for class.

A bodywash gel company created the advertisement. She was amazed at how simple it was for her to obtain, but when she got there, she discovered that she was only at the rear of the advertisement. She didn't realize she didn't win anything significant. Her level of polish is lacking. She understood that many had tried hard and yet failed, so she didn't feel all that horrible. She was okay with it, too, since she was in the rear. She remained silent while observing everyone at work. Thanks to social media, she learned about that. There, she was well-known. She was conflicted when she heard this. Even so, she puts on makeup, dresses, and records herself. When she looked in the mirror, she felt content. She simply followed the instructions that everyone gave her. Because she was worried about getting reprimanded, she didn't complain or make any requests. Since she wasn't the major role, she didn't make a mistake on her first shoot. Her performance was not very important. That why she didn't have to put a lot of work.

She didn't like the food after it was all through and had a look around. However, she indulges in ice cream for herself. Sweet treat.

When she got home. Her father did not answer the ring when she rang it. She considered the possibility that his government residents may prevent him from returning home today. She opened the door with the keys she took out of her backpack.

Danish appeared from behind, and she became alarmed. He held a spoon and said, "Come here, we are having dinner." He gave her a spoon as well. She closed her eyes and murmured, "You scared me." "I apologize; I didn't mean to."

She entered his house. And she observed everyone seated at the dining table for dinner. She was not in the mood to sit there; instead, she planned to come up with an excuse to watch TV on the couch. She was not interested in having family conversations. She was shoved toward the dinner table by Danish. She sat there, unable to resist. She hurried to the kitchen to grab something in between. Although it wasn't serious, she believed there was.

The Danish's mother seems quite thrilled, saying, "I have told everyone, but many of us were waiting for Danish to get a job in California, and we are celebrating." She turns to face the smiling Danish. She was pleased with him. "We shall be apart, but I'm glad he'll be accomplishing something amazing," his father grinned when his mother delivered the bad news. Danish remained silent, a little anxious at being apart from everyone. He has been here all along. He seldom spends more than a month living alone, although obstacles will arise as circumstances change. Moreover, Manya's father was pleased. He was glad to see that, although he had taught him a lot in the past, he was now succeeding.

Manya was taken aback by his early employment offer; she had assumed he would stay longer. However, he was with them for a few months. She congratulated him, beaming with happiness. Running, she grabbed the fake flower from the pot. And she gave him a laugh that made everyone laugh. "I was hoping you would stay a little longer, but it's still awesome," she remarked, delighted that he was pursuing his dream. Manya's father stated, "It's the right time for him; he will learn a lot there." Danish was a little anxious to leave things behind, but everyone was thrilled for him. He was under the impression that his parents might visit while on vacation, but he is aware that they will be alone elsewhere. They are likewise unable to quit their occupations.

"Manya, where were you?" Danish's father enquired. She has remained quiet and has been hesitant to disclose her auditions to others. Danish had earlier informed her, "She tried out for an advertisement and got that part, but it was her first time." She remained silent and continued eating because she felt ashamed. His mother tells her, "Oh nice, finally you started auditioning; you will get roles easily." She continues to nod. She gives her father a glance. He appeared disinterested in what was being said. She didn't want to talk about it, so she disregarded it.

"Why are you doing advertisements when your dream is to become an actor?" Her father enquired. Manya did not know what to say about her lack of a plan—she was just going for the experience—and her lack of direction. Her words ran out.

She shook and said, "I just did it simple."

"How basic," he remarked nonchalantly.

Danish speak up as it was he who recommended the audition. "I suggested she did it," He stopped asking questions after hearing that. She was shocked that it would be okay just because Danish said so. "How come you despise me?" With her head down, she murmured, "All my decisions feel wrong to you," and she stopped eating. Her emotions were out of control. Danish made an attempt to stop them because he sensed horrible was about to happen. Speaking a little louder, he declares, "I don't hate; you think like that; if I hated you, I wouldn't let you do this." Danish's parents attempt to soothe him. "Why do you make fun of me every day then? This brings shame to me." She apologizes for making Danish day worse, tears welling up in her eyes. She climbed to her feet, grabbed her purse, and left. Slammed the door. All were silent, tears welling up in her father's eyes. Danish head out to locate her.

Their Cold War anxiety plagued Manya and her father constantly. They endured like this arguing amongst themselves instead of finding such a solution to their difficulties. They have to make their ritual, so even when they agree on something, they usually end up fighting. This time, they incited a brawl on a Danish employment day. Though it wasn't much, they won't speak for perhaps a week after this. This is a constant occurrence. They have been disregarding the issue and continuing to live this way as Manya grows older.

Manya did not travel far; she was located at the corner park, making her unfindable. She could see Danish approaching; she needed to escape since she was weeping. She tried to stay away from him. She ignored him when he tried to stop her. She didn't want to raise a scene with certain folks, so she went home. Danish went after her. "Manya, pay attention," he said as he walked in, but she retreated to her room and shut the door. He did not know what to do. She realizes her mistake and opens the door within the following two minutes. "I apologize for ruining your day; it was yours. I'm doing okay, don't worry, you can leave now," came the abrupt shift in thinking. She felt bad because he wasn't deserving of this and was making things difficult for him. To avoid making matters worse, she decided to shift her mind in favour of him. He was relieved that she wasn't crying, even though she still had a tear in her eyes. Nonetheless, he stayed put.

She was seated on the floor next to the bed when he entered her room. Now look better. She grinned at him, said she was sorry. She feels disorganized. No one will contest it. "It's alright". Sitting next to her, he continued, "Many things take time, and you are in college; you get things if you work hard." She begins to cry once more. "It's not why he can't be happy with me; I'm angry because of that."

Danish are aware that no matter how much he explains, she will never get it. She needs to speak with her dad. For a few minutes, they remain silent as Manya is unwilling to speak. She started crying. He touched her shoulder with his hand. They sat side by side till her tears ceased. He added, "You need to talk to him; only the two of you can solve the problem." Without ado. She realized he was correct. A long, long quiet of perhaps twenty minutes fell. All she could do was stare at the wall.

She posed a surprising question out of the blue, "Since you like me," which made Danish freeze. He understands what she's trying to express, but he was also perplexed when she asked, "What are you trying to say?" He responded coolly. They awkwardly face each other while grinning. "I apologize for speaking so quickly; I saw tears in your eyes and had to say something," she later stated with sorrow. He genuinely said, "I was never going to say it, so it's okay that you said it."

"Why is it the case?" They never communicate with each other in this way, so she felt strange. "You are aware of it, so why would I mention anything about myself that would offend you? Is it not reasonable to inquire? It's best not to bother; after all, but I always treated the same like always" He was unable to look someone in the eye.

"Sure, you're always nice to me, but why do you always push yourself to form connections with other people?" She wanted to know why he kept it so secret.

"I thought you would be with someone else, which would have made things easier, but you never stick with someone; your relationships never work out like mine," he stammers.

She was anger, "I knew it always; all the girls left you because of me. How is that possible for someone?"

"Everyone continuously asks me to keep my distance from you, but I couldn't make them feel uneasy; that's not others fault. It was my decision."

"Why do they think that I would end your relationship?"

"They know me as well as you; it was me, not you, that caused the issue."

Manya stopped talking. She was unable to continue. A calmer Danish than she was enrage. "Remember, this is the best thing I can do to focus on things; it's like starting a new life that will be fun. Think like this: I am going to the U.S.; you will find someone; maybe I will. Don't worry, I am not angry with you. I can't force you." He encourages her and himself. "I am destroying your day," she said, apologizing recently but staying loyal to those who mattered most. It was alright with him. At least now that they were closer, he thought it would be best to keep everything that was suffocating him a secret.

❧❧❧

The issue between Manya and her father was not resolved, but they did have an unfavourable automatic conversation. They both believed that ego outweighed problem-solving skills. They were living apart at the time, but it didn't bother them. Although the advertising was overly brief, Manya was pleased to see her in it, so she told her father about it. She was a little ashamed that there wasn't much, but she still wanted to show everyone. She therefore chose to display solely Danish. The issue is that he has been largely ignoring her for a number of days. He said that while he wouldn't be seeing Manya anymore, he would be at ease and calm about it. All he did was text her; he never even came home. Despite her insistence, Manya believes he is going to leave soon. If nothing else, they ought to treat each other well.

Entering his room, she went. He had his desk open and working. He was drinking water first, then juice.

"Water after juice is unhealthy," she remarked, glancing away. "Does it result in demise?" He didn't move. "No," she said, annoyed at his response. "It's okay then."

She held her phone out in front of him right away. "Where are you?", pretending not to have noticed it. She displayed it again after reversing it. He was at a loss for words, saying only, "Oh nice." Her phone went into her pocket. "You begin acting strangely," she gave him a fierce look. She was about to attack him, but he backed off, saying, "Maybe I don't know, but I am trying."

CHAPTER NINE

Manya tried again during the audition, but this time she didn't obtain any roles. Nevertheless, everyone advised her to keep trying. She occasionally was unable to attend due to college-related activities. Her goal on social media is to stay engaged. She is rather well-liked there. Folks adore her humorous stuff.

It was a pink midi dress on Manya. It's colourful on her. She waited for her father to arrive so she could get out, but he never showed up. She reserved the taxi. She saw Danish before their scheduled meeting, but she didn't say anything to her. It bothered her that their relationship had changed just a few days. Her taxi showed up. Her father didn't answer the phone when she called.

She arrived at the eatery, which also has a club. She understands that she neglected to enjoy herself outside by spending so much time concentrating on her college education. She used to go out a lot when she was in school. Although she didn't find school to be all that tough, she now fears what would happen to her if she doesn't succeed. She becomes competitive because of how much competition there is in college.

When her phone rang, Kartik answered. Even though he was in front of her, she knew who he was. He came to her when she spotted him. Kartik found it awkward, while Manya didn't find it awkward. He was conversing with her less than he had in the past. They were conversing and had lengthy talks for a number of days. He no longer makes as much fun of her, and they now value opinions and counsel. They spend a lot of time together at college. They were talking about the show they were trying to audition for. And for that reason, he is picking up direction. The night was a Saturday, and every club was packed. Reaching the bar was a battle for them. The entire club exuded Punjabi vibes. Manya begins to talk in Punjabi. Kartik was unable to comprehend anything. He thought it was easy but when she get difficult with words he couldn't get it. She did say a few words to him. Kartik fell silent once more, and Manya could not stop talking.

"Why do I feel like you're so far away some days? You don't even come, so serious, focusing on your profession," she said with a sly smile before sipping her drink. He's been working, which is why they converse a lot on social media. "I'm okay, maybe I'm just changing," he says with an inane smile. Manya had a hunch that Kartik had perhaps altered since his behaviour and eyes had changed a few days prior. She now finds him to be a better, more sensible guy who doesn't irritate her. But she's reluctant to speak because of her previous encounter. It still bothered her, even if she allowed herself to love it. She refrained from asking inquiries despite her insatiable curiosity.

"You reject Yash, but why?" Suddenly, he starts questioning her. She took a silent moment to consider what to say. "How are you aware of that? Who informed you? I think Shresth is guilty." In the end, he admits, "It is obvious I saw him; actually, I asked him." He made a fool of her, but she was surprised he could tell him. "That is what he agreed to," she murmured, still in disbelief. She grew perplexed and answered, "No, he refuse to admit that he like me; he made it look like I was desperate." Yash was ignoring her while making strange remarks. "It seems like I am a fool, but I don't understand anything." Rewind everything in her head.

"Really, you don't like him?" He shifted the subject.

She was attempting to clarify, saying, "I don't hate him, but I don't feel anything about him."

"What do you like then?" he persisted in asking. Manya turn to consider what he is attempting to convey. He was putting bombs on her, and she didn't want to answer him, so she decided to ignore him. She chuckled and said, "I like people who don't like me," but he was still curious. Her eyes had so much going on that it struck his eyes. Manya never paid that much attention to him. The answer is constantly changing, so really, she have no idea. That's the thing she find confusing. She considered Yash's comment, but she avoided making eye contact.

"So I have to dislike you"

"No, perhaps someone matured." She was unable to look him in the eyes because of the way he was looking. He smiled and nodded. His face and look had completely changed. Manya can see that, but Kartik was reluctant to acknowledge it. He loves being with her now.

"Shall we go out to dance together?" He queries the throng. She didn't start dancing, but she did stand there. She noticed that a lot of buddies and couples were making out. With others, Kartik begins to step in. Manya make fun of him. He readily gets along with new people. Kartik encouraged her to dance, saying, "I don't know this dance," but she refused. Perhaps she forgot to have fun. "You are capable of performing Kathak here," Kartik said in a direct and quiet manner. With a backward shove, she burst out laughing. He started the Kathak dance. "This is completely incorrect," she corrected him. She eventually joined as well. She gave her hair a quick shake from right to left to left, joking around. Taking her hair behind her hands, Kartik tucked it behind her back. That makes them tense with each other. She comes to a stop.

Manya began to grow weary. She was heading to the dining area. In order to stay, Kartik grasped her hand. "Leaving now, I want to eat. And I cannot eat by myself."

Manya stood there and he wanted to pause, "I want to say something." Her tummy tingles a little when she listens. She desires both to listen and to lose herself in the music.

"You're not fond of the eatery."

"No"

"You don't feel like eating right now."

"Oh, no, it just simple but I like you, that's what I want to say," he muttered, shattering the quiet in the most audible location, but Manya went blank and continued to display her strange expression. He expresses his dissatisfaction, but it should be in a beautiful way. She wanted rewind the moment so that she could listen. The sound was so loud. "Yes, you are also good," she remarked, raising her voice to his attention. "You have time to respond; you don't have to right now."

Manya drunk slept in late. She was lightheaded due to a hangover, but she woke up when Kartik said something and unintentionally ran into her dream. Her father shouted. She refuses to come out of her room. She gives a quick peek outside. Perhaps he left. She recalls meeting her dad while intoxicated; although he didn't yell, she could tell he was upset with her. She simply doesn't want to meet in this manner, even though she remembers everything. She emerged in her jammies right away.

It was hunger driving her crazy. She was hoping for something hot, but nothing came of it. She fled to Danish house. She rang the bell briskly. He yelled, "Coming." When she saw her father at his house, her attitude instantly soured. She didn't consider this possibility. She refused to enter, standing at the doorway. Danish hit her face with the door slam. He remarked as he opened the door once more, "Do you want to come or I'll do that again?" Though she wanted to hide, she entered beaming. She was summoned to the table by all. She grabbed a dish from the kitchen, rushed, and sat on her tiptoes. After adding onion, chilly, and lemon to some poha, she added a generous amount of aloo bhujia. She was about to take her first bite when she looked up into her father's somewhat irate face. He declined her offer of one spoon.

He puts a half-lemon with seeds in it and says, "Put some more lemon; it will cure your hangover." She expels the lemon. She made a dramatic face while eating it even though it turned sour. "Now we're off again," she murmured, fully aware of what was ahead. Danish was unaware of it, nor was his family. They seem inquisitive. Without even asking what it was, he said, "What have you done again?" He believes Manya will be the one. He believes no one is more adept at making mistakes than her.

She looked down and remarked, "I am living my life, and he has problems." She was consuming bites one after the other without even trying to finish the last one. She wishes she could go sooner. Everyone attempts to calm him down, but he looks irritated. "Life doesn't mean dating every guy; I am not saying to live; I am just saying there is some moral in life," he says.

He lives by a set of rules that he believes will help him have a wonderful life. Manya has ideas of her own that conflict with what he is trying to educate her. "She is young, and she is not the one who injured someone." They become perplexed. Danish's mother attempts to save her, but nothing works. It is preferable for her to remain silent. He said, "She took an expensive restaurant," which shocked everyone because Manya is not a frequent spender of money. Being the youngest in the family, she is aware that someone will eventually spend money for her, which is why she doesn't spend it readily. Surprising her as well, the Danish's father said, "That's unexpected, but it's fine to spend some money," while laughing. Her father disagreed with his friend. "You're encouraging her now." It causes two long-time friends to argue. Danish was the only one who was relaxed at that particular moment. He was simply listening to Manya, who he knew quite well. He is aware of her movement and actions. But he made no attempt to clarify the circumstances.

"Why are you suddenly interested in me?, You have no idea what kind of boys I don't like," Manya says, trying to change the subject.

"What kind of inquiry is this?" He added, "I mean, I think maybe introvert." Still answered.

"No, terrible humour," Manya and Danish echoed each other, adding that she didn't appreciate that he cut her off in the middle of their talk. She looked at him. "What I do, I was quiet before," he says, expressing a preference for solitude.

The Danish parent attempted to cut the talk short by saying, "I don't understand this generation, but I think she'll figure things out on her own."

"I don't know what kind of guys you like, but I'm aware that I don't allow meeting people at random on the night out. You're growing up and becoming responsible for yourself, and I don't want to watch you go out and find people late at night," he firmly said. The nonserious Danish guy laughed a little in the middle, but he spoke as little as he could considering how serious the subject was. Manya did nothing except nod.

Manya was attempting to go asleep when she started watching a television show that was about Indian family dramas, which she wasn't really into. She can't relate to things because her family isn't complete. She leaps from her bed and pulls open the drawer containing her old pictures. She turns her mother's pictures over one by one. She doesn't miss her, therefore she doesn't get emotional when she sees her. She was raised by her father and has lived with him ever since. She is unaware of the distinction between being with and being without her. It was a fairly easy divorce for them. She had her granny raise her. When she was a sixth grader, she passed away. Her heart broke so much over it. Although she couldn't comprehend the idea of death, she could still understand it. She and her grandmother used to watch a lot of movies together. Together, they watched a ton of Indian films. She also utilized to clarify the director's points of view. Her other dream was to become an actor, but in those days, being an actress in the entertainment business was considered derogatory. She did, however, demonstrate how Indian actors established themselves and rose to fame. She selected the theatre for this reason. She desires to go through it all.

She occasionally looks through her photo album to see how things were and where she is now. She observes her parents' struggles and separation. Although she wasn't opposed to relationships, she found it difficult to form bonds with other individuals. She invariably causes harm to others. She lacks the time and knowledge necessary to act appropriately in a relationship. She is handled like a friend by her.

She pauses at her parents' picture and prays for the courage to build enduring relationships. She dated a few males, but their relationships were always quite brief. She doesn't seem to take other people seriously, doesn't communicate, and forgets things. When they are tired, they leave. She is also unaffected by that. Even so, she is aware of her issue, but she makes no effort to address it. She is surrounded by people today, therefore she is feeling emotionless. She wants to start dating right away, but once more, she is afraid of messing things up. Kartik has been sweet to her; she feels somewhat content with him. She was simply unable to come up with a suitable response. She wants it, but her self-awareness makes her fearful. The fact that she didn't immediately reject it made her feel like something. She had previously said no without hesitation and never regretted it. She was thinking, though, this time.

Manya is having trouble with the paper that she turned in to the office. She's been sluggish for several days because she couldn't give up, but now she understands the urgency. She didn't know which way she needed to go. She reached the office somehow and was waiting in line. He shuts the window and refuses to accept her submission of the document. "We don't accept it now because you are late," he remarked, pointing to her document.

Uncertain on what to do, she stood there. They locked all the countertops once she moved to the next one, where everyone was eating mango. She was noticed by the guard. "You may exit through the rear entrance." He didn't appear particularly kind when assisting pupils, but he did. She entered the workplace. The old paper was never shown to her. Everything was vintage and old. "How did you get in here?" inquired the counterman. "The guard indicated that I could enter," she shakily says. "Give me the documents, please," he said. She didn't believe it would be so simple, but he accepted the document without arguing. While he was going over the paperwork, Manya was just glancing about.

"So much paper here, could be valuable for garbage seller, sir," she remarked.

The way he didn't even give her a glance. She complimented him, saying, "You people don't use computers; everything is on paper," but it seemed insulting to him. He took off his glasses. "We make use of PCs. This is from a computer that I am sending it to you," he stated. He gave her the paper without giving her a glance.

She left, muttering to herself that she makes mistakes all the time. However, she is happy that her labour is done. Danish bike caught her attention on the approach to her section. She didn't know his bike number, but it was the engineering department. He continued to appear like that. Everyone in the department turned to stare at her when she walked in because she didn't look recognizable to them. She checks herself to see whether she is looking strange while still staring at them. She sensed his voice, but she was unsure of its source. She listened in from outside the classroom. When she saw him, she said, "Danish," quite loudly. She looked through each class before locating him. The thing that seemed strange was that he was apparently lecturing other people. She is unable to understand what he has written. Everyone turns their focus to Manya. "Why does a girl suddenly jump into our class, I wonder?" When she noticed that she was slowing down and backing off. Reducing the tension, he says, "Don't worry, she's my childhood friend; she just got excited." Everyone synchronized exclaimed, "Oh."

She left the classroom. Her back was to the wall. He briefly emerged and stated, "It's okay you do this every day; this happened to me; nothing to embarrass." She simply nodded while glancing at the ground. "You and I shall meet after this." Saying, "I call you," she hurried to the classroom. There was a waiting list for him.

Danish called all the time, but she didn't answer. She was simply dozing off in the movie with her phone on quiet, as if she were upset about something. After becoming irate, he went into the department. Where to go, he did not know. He was only glancing around while carrying a bulky luggage. From time to time, he was switching the sides, from left to right. He rested by sitting on the stairs. "Are you in the class?" he writes, pulling out his phone. "Either way, I'm leaving." And he got up. Manya ran over; there was a door next to the stairs. Her eyes dart left and right.

Angrily, he remarked, "I don't know why I listened to you and waited; I meet you every day."

Suddenly hitting him in the shoulder, she apologized, saying, "I didn't tell you to wait, but still, I got into sleep." He said, "I want to eat something in the canteen," as he continued to consider other options. "Don't try this here; I'll tell you it's bad."

Hoping she would find some nice cuisine, he followed her. His gaze was searching; he always arrived and left more quickly. Manya is well-known to all. She actually greeted everyone with a hello. Kartik appeared, squinting at her head. He chuckled. Quiet Danish was behind. One can see the other. She understands, "He is my friend," as Kartik appears to be inquiring. She was accurate. They had an awkward greeting. The strange thing emerged from behind Shresth, Niti, and Yash.

Yash was with them. They just gave him the assignment. The college project is a great way to meet people, but it can also lead to arguments. Everybody just stood there, staring at the ravenous Danish face. "I am Danish, and I am not affiliated with your college," he stated during his preamble. Danish knew everyone and their tale, therefore he didn't need names. He remembers them in his head as they utter their names. To be honest, he never really intended to be friends with a lot of his pals. He finds it awkward every time. Be away is preferable. He remained quiet as they conversed. Danish were only troubled by hunger. They were heading out because he wanted to eat something. "Want to come along?" Danish was happy to learn that others was hungry too, but she didn't like the thought of them approaching. He was feeling bad about the choice he had made; he should have gone home to fetch the food and missed the meeting. When they concur, Danish is let down.

She proceeded to the Bhelpuri booth. So that he might at least have something, she took first. Danish wanted something meaningful, so he was surprised. "You think this will be enough for me?" he asks, glancing away to focus on something else. He remained silent so as not to come across as a picky eater. He consumed two bhelpuri in a paper cone throughout that period. He simply ate without saying anything. Each of them had one. Up to the Pani Puri stall, they stroll. All of them had pani puri, but not Shresth, who couldn't take the spiciness. For the aloo chaat, they wait. Danish had more enthusiasm. He went to help others before taking his own.

Shresth says, "What are you doing right now?" To facilitate communication, they took a circle seat on a circular chair. "I am a developer I completed my software engineering degree that time I was working still continuing." He spoke more focused on the food when he remarked, "I'm going to the USA to work after some time." To fetch more onions, he gets up. Manya concludes by summarizing what he has already taught them. Manya made fun of him, saying, "He is our enemy; he is a scholar; don't ask him; he will flex; he came to college today for debate and lecture."

"I am not a threat to anyone," he declared. Everybody was in awe of him. His future seems to be quite clear. "Your artwork appears impressive," Niti remarks. Still, Danish was unable to concede that he lived a happy existence. He must always be visible on the front screen. A single error may turn out to be a major issue. For his career, he literally studied a ton, and he made a lot of mistakes in his practice. He was employed by numerous persons but never received pay. Still, he works through the night, compromising his sleep. People comment in the end, "Wow, your life is great." He has to put in a lot of work despite being in a favourable position.

He remarked, "My life is fine; it stinks like everyone," but he made no effort to clarify his meaning to others. To believe like them is preferable to him; let them do. "Are you friends from school?" Yash and Kartik inquire. They are both very curious yet unable to ask many inquiries. Danish had no desire to converse extensively. "Maybe since we were born because his father and my father are friends," she chuckles. It's been so long for them that they are unaware of it. Once more, everyone was in awe.

She gave them an update on her family and him. "You have to battle a lot," Kartik remarked, eager to learn. It appears that Yash and Kartik are becoming envious. Danish didn't want to meet her pals because he knew that people sometimes feel embarrassed about their friendships. "I don't fight; he does," Manya yells. After getting to know her for a few months, Shresth said, "I don't think like this definitely could be you." The spoon fell from Manya's grasp and caught her jeans. Kartik gets her a tissue, which looks fine, but he cleansed the spot himself, not because he got the tissue. He made a gesture that stunned everyone. He remained expressionless. She got some more tissues from him. Danish merely gave her a smile. Yash had a more animated countenance. His smile vanished, but he was unable to hide.

Danish phone rang. He replaced the plate. He had to finish his task before leaving, so he went to speak. He had to return home. When he remarked, "Sorry, I have to go home; see you next time," he wasn't exactly saying what people generally say. He turned to go, then halted. "Since Manya's birthday is approaching, her dad normally throws a lunch party." He responds, "You all should come," understanding that her father will never turn him down. This did not sit well with Manya, who preferred that her father not get to know her friends. It was too late for her to refuse. "Yes, you all should come." With excitement, he said, "It will be fine; make sure you all come." It is unclear to Manya why. They would try, but they didn't immediately say they agreed.

CHAPTER TEN

Manya chose to roam around the entire store by saying, "This one, this one, this one, and this one, pack all." Danish merely shot her a sidelong glance. Several items asked for to be returned as gifts for all of her friends, and he was purchasing for the US. "What money do you even have?" She had taken the money out of her pocket, but he could see that she didn't have any. Her gift-giving was restricted. "It's fine, I'll pay you today," he added, a little hesitant. That she'll buy whole shop now.

"No, I have money; you don't have to pay."

"I'm leaving soon, but I might not return later."

"You just want to say that you're leaving, huh?"

To choose the chocolate, she took a seat on the ground. A boy was vlogging in the store, saying, "I'm in an Indian grocery store; Indian chocolate are more sweeter than usual." He may have purchased something to meet a challenge. It dawned on her that he was looking for the spicier items. Gazing at him, she grinned. "Which chocolates have chilly in it?" Manya became disgusted with him at the moment he was saying this. "No," she said with such emotion that he could see why you asked me this. She needs to think about this. "Oh, I would like that favour," she stated, brushing off his remark. She got up. And unintentionally enter his frame. Giving a different chocolate.

He asks, putting the camera in his face, "You can get in video; I am making a vlog." He was unable to speak as she was just focusing on his camera. "Hello" is all she can think of. Her silence prompted him to end the video.

"It's not what you want to say, Don't be scared."

"Yes, I'm sorry"

"Oh, that need not be. In fact, I just travelled to India and did some exploring. What cuisine is available here?"

"Obviously, Pav Bhaji is well-known from here, down the next lane; you can try."

"How am I going to cover the entire place?" He was referring to a location on his phone.

He was writing when she said, "You cannot cover them all; you can do some of them."

"What is your phone number, please? I will speak with you. You may also appear in the video."

She didn't give it much thought, but she felt a little uncomfortable providing the number to a complete stranger, as he mentioned. Danish had finished buying groceries. She didn't alter, even though he was disappointed that she might be in danger when he noticed that she was providing a number. "Where were you when I was waiting?" In an attempt to be courteous, he says. In an attempt to break free from the interaction with her, he grasped her hand. "Who is he, I wonder?" He poses the query. Danish was intrigued about Manya and was shocked to learn that she didn't even know him. He seemed agitated. "I'm her boyfriend," he said, not wanting to continue the conversation and escorting her outside right away. She was pressed for time and said nothing.

"How come you said that?" She withdrew her hand.

After recognizing they should slow down, they started fighting in the middle of the road. "It doesn't become real; I just bother about why you give a stranger your number," he said. All eyes were on them. She continued, "I know I shouldn't give him, but he looks genuine," but she was at a loss for words. She just does it without giving it any thought. "It may be risky, but alright, everyone has come, let's head home." Much obliged to wait. They both know they might be running late. They carry the bag and ran.

Outside the apartment, Kartik, Yash, and Shresth were waiting. Their phones were occupied while they sat on the swing together. They were still swinging quickly. "At last, she's here," Shresth exclaimed, getting to his feet first. Yash had become weary of holding out. To her he ran. "Where did you go?" She looked at Danish first. "I was buying something," she stammered out. Kartik cuts you off. "It isn't too late," Kartik remarked. Danish was like why he always have to say something. He want to just shut his mouth.

Manya's father was the reason for everyone's anxiety. What type of party is this, Manya wondered. She intended to throw them a separate, authentic celebration as part of her strategy. Nevertheless, she doesn't believe she dates at random and believes it will be beneficial for her father to meet her friends. He will consider her to be quite talkative.

Her father decide to throw party at the government residence. It was quite spacious then her flat. When Danish rang the bell, gifts were being given to everyone behind him. Her father opened the door, something he doesn't do very often. His attempt was to be a gracious host. "Come on in, all of you." As he stood at the threshold, everyone gave him the namaste greeting. Manya did as well. He glanced over to one side. They take a seat on the couch.

However, Manya came to a stop when she noticed her mother waiting to give her a hug. She was taken aback that she failed to pay her a visit. Her mother grabbed her right away and gave her a hug, knowing she would be asking a lot of questions. Danish was astounded as well because he hadn't anticipated this. It pleased his parents, too, to see them together again. Manya didn't appear too joyful. There was guy standing the same youngster she had met in the grocery store, and her mother said, "He is my son, Ritwik." He emerged from the restroom. They each gave each other a shocked look. She was receiving surprises one after another, which is why she was so astonished. Danish approached him more closely. He gave him a hug. "I had no idea," he was unable to say.

Her mother arrived to introduce her, saying, "I never got the chance to tell; now I thought you would meet and get along." Manya recognized that everyone was present and she didn't want any family drama to occur, so she just grinned awkwardly. Danish said, "First, let's just eat; I'm heating the food." He is not interested in them speaking more. Since her dad has follower but still want to dodge the dramatic reunion. Though uncomfortable, Manya's father made an effort to ensure everyone was at ease. He asks them about their plans and what they want to do in the future.

"Why wasn't Niti here?" her father enquired. He had everyone in memory. That he was thoughtful of them astounded Shresth. "I'll give her a call." She tried calling her number, but she didn't answer. Manya was trying, though.

"You didn't show up; we didn't really get started."

She was lying when she said, "I cannot come, I have some much work, but happy birthday." She and her partner were in Delhi. There's nothing for her to do. She was still technically unable to attend. Nor did Manya coerce her into coming.

"I had no idea you were an officer," Yash said, expressing her fascination with him. There are differences in the characters of Manya and her father. They don't appear to be a father and daughter team. He posed and appeared more composed. Manya is also obnoxious and unclear. "To be honest, I've always wanted to be an officer." It was unexpected that Manya's father was well-liked by all; they discussed his hardships and academic methods. Danish's father share their strategies for running to their joint college, providing coaching, and managing finances. It didn't feel like Manya's birthday. Despite her desire to ignore her mother, she was unable to focus on eating. She sampled some biryani. Danish says, "Hey, you should wait for everyone." She took a tissue, spit in it and gave it to Danish. "This is what?" It disgusted him. "It's open for you to see," she muttered. Grinning broadly at everyone, he got up to toss.

"Remember that this is not a pleasant surprise, you were hitting on me." She remarked, "When I don't know you, so just shut up," when she noticed Ritwik, her new brother, was creating a vlog once more. She moved to face the camera. He continues to record the footage while saying, "You are blocking my way." Her statement, "I am older, and I say not to make a video without my permission," grabs everyone's interest. She responded clumsily, "I mean, we should enjoy the food; we can talk later."

She serves everyone and forgets about stuff. Manya has the ability to forget things very easily, which can be advantageous and disadvantageous depending on the situation. "I was a little worried that we would be meeting the first you," Yash said to Manya's father when she forgot to do something. His generosity left them speechless. "This isn't the first time I've met Kartik," said the pleasant party host but nasty gossip. Shresth sniffs. He gives her a glint. Danish remained silent because he was always aware of the situation. He is somehow aware of her life events. That much was clear to him. But does this affect him?, yes a lot. Kartik says, "I'm sorry, I couldn't meet you properly that day." Without extending his hand, he answered, "No, it's okay; you were having fun on Saturday."

Manya's mother eventually admits, "You only vibe with guys," but she only chooses catastrophe. About her term "Vibe," the younger generation is more peculiar. Perhaps she's been living in Italy for a while with her kid, which Manya finds few year earlier. She was more Manya-like previously, but now she's altered drastically. She is now Damini. The Danish's mother remarked, "She always has better friendships with men; it's maybe a coincidence, see Danish. She take her friendship seriously." She was there to pardon her at all times. She grinned.

"In actuality, she has poor communication skills," Danish people believe in confrontations.

She smirks, "My communication is not that bad; actually, I am rude." Danish was taken aback by her remarks. "Well, she's right after all," Manya's father says to end the discussion.

He rises and retrieves the cake. He set it down on the surface. He stroked a few candles. So that he wouldn't have to be with her mother, Manya herself came. Yash had a party bomber ready. While slicing the cake. He blew up the bomber party.

"Who will clean this, though?" Manya's lips dropped open in disappointment. Not only was she not slicing the cake. "Just cut the cake; I'll clean," Danish shoved her hand. Though it's always unpleasant to eat into someone else's food first, she went with her father. She always chooses him, even when they argue. She then decided on Danish's parents. The older one worked better. Danish chose cream and cheerfully placed her nose in his hand. "I must snap a photo," she yelled at him. It surprised him. Instead of retaliating, she put the cake on the plates. As she accepted the platter, her mother grinned to see her.

Manya visits her buddies in company. "I am really sorry I called you all to my home; we should have gone somewhere else," she said as soon as she left the bungalow. Yash is longing for food. He opened his returned gift and removed the chocolate. He consumed it all at once. Kartik's reply, "You don't have to be sorry; just blame it on Danish," sounded more like bigotry. Yash nods, his mouth full of chocolate. Everyone is able to perceive their hatred at this moment.

"To be honest, I enjoy spending time with your crazy family," Yash concludes. "That's my life's privilege," she declared, her expression disgusted. After a period of conversation, Kartik fell silent and fixed his gaze on Manya as though he was waiting for something. Their gazes locked, but neither spoke. Manya understands she must respond to him. Even though she remained puzzled, she was making an effort to put her family out of her thoughts so that she could concentrate on herself. "Let's go," Yash says, although he doesn't want to because Kartik was starting to bother him. He hid a lot of things that he was embarrassed to say but was unable to express.

Manya's mother was narrating her story with great enthusiasm. She was the successful owner of a fabric manufacturing company. They didn't even inquire, so she talked about her factor's entire process. Although Manya's father doesn't want to talk much, he was fine with her ex-wife living with her daughter. With so many of her friends gone, he fell silent. He went into the kitchen to prepare masala lime soda, trying to ignore her. Danish went after him. He was loading the refrigerator with leftovers.

"Do you feel uncomfortable?" Danish was positioned across from him. He remarked softly that no one could hear them. However, after hearing his query, he paused briefly before responding. He continued, not even turning to face him, "Yes, of course, I know Manya also doesn't like it, but he thought she was her biological mother and couldn't deny her." Staying silent was preferable to asking more questions, in his opinion.

He abruptly moved aside and said, "Manya is very famous in her college; I didn't know."

"Yes, she is."

"When you knew they liked her, why did you call them?"

Danish eyes, shocked, were wide open. He doesn't usually say stuff like this, so he wasn't even prepared for it. "No, it's not in the three," he interrupted him. "Yeah, I only know Kartik and Yash; and you, eyes tell you everything," he laughed. "But this wasn't the question I was asking."

He answers, "What do you mean?" and picks up his work quickly so he may go out of the kitchen. He picked up the glass and filled it with masala. "Why are you acting so fake when I know you like her?" He attempted to look Danish in the eye, but Danish did not glance up. His gaze enlarges. Even from the Manya's perspective, it was hard for him because he is her father and he doesn't want to defy him. He was considering his response. When is it permissible to say "yes" or "no"? He touched his shoulder with his hand. "It's okay, even though I know you don't want to say anything. I am aware that Manya dislikes you." Danish put his palm to his face in embarrassment. "How are you so knowledgeable?" He completely disregards limeade. "I thought you might know that Manya thinks the way she does, but I can understand that." Before serving, he poured soda into each glass. It dawned to him that Danish was not coming. He returned to give him a call.

"I apologize, Danish. I surprised you in this way," he murmured as he stood in front of him.

He was dejected about leaving and felt conflicted. "No, no, you don't have to be; actually, it's just hit me that growing up should be fun, but it's going terrible," he replied.

"So, have fun with it; you have to feel good; others can't."

Both of them laughed, "And it's really weird to talk to you like this."

❧❧❧

"I've heard you aspire to be an actress," Manya and Ritwik said as they sat down to talk more. Danish himself started to stray from the topic. "Oh, I'm studying that," she answered, sounding a little impolite. Danish muttered, "Don't be harsh; he doesn't like you." Ritwik made an effort to listen, but he was unable to do so, and he is undoubtedly unhappy with Manya's actions. "And he's not my boyfriend," Manya remarked abruptly. He burst out laughing. "I can see well; you don't have to tell me that." Danish gave Manya a quick spin. He wishes to avoid discussing it further. He is an industrious individual who, rather than feeling ashamed, frequently impresses people. He made sure to accentuate every phrase, "And I wasn't flirting with you; I actually want to try the food from here."

"Do yourself, then. I need to head to college."

They both gang up and deny, saying, "And I am leaving soon, so I have lots of work."

"However, I can compile a list of places you can try."

"Amazing, giving to my sibling," he grinned, but Manya tapped him on the feet.

Manya's mother abruptly interrupted the discussion to approach Manya. She pulled out a box from her purse. Placed it upon the table. Manya said, "It's too costly; I can't take it," without even looking at the contents of the package. Although it appears to be a box necklace, she is unsure if it would be inexpensive. For her, her mother unlocked the package. That was secured. Manya stared at the adorable locket. Somewhere, she believes herself to be respectable; she doesn't want to deny it.

"Accept it," Ritwik murmured. Danish gave a doubtful nod. She said, "It's okay, I don't need this. Thank you for coming," as she closed the box and handed it to her. She affirms to her father that her actions were correct. She's amused that she's right; he seems proud. Her mom didn't coerce her once more.

With her in her seat. "I'm very excited for you in the professional world, my friend has been told about you, and she plans to give you a call soon." They become the centre of attention. She add on. "She is a casting director." Although they are aware that Manya dislikes to converse, her mother still gets upset when she sees her after all these years. That Manya doesn't share such feelings is strange. She's grown more and more aloof from her over time, and she simply doesn't care about her anymore.

She added gently, "You don't have to worry so much; I am learning right now." The silence was deafening. "There is a lot of struggle in your work. Many people are talented, yet they are not successful." She goes on, "You also need other things." Manya remained silent, but her expression conveys a lot.

"I understand that you attended my birthday, but please just let me be myself. You didn't pick me, and I didn't choose to be so annoying that you forgot when I was hurt and was in the hospital," she cries. She said what she was thinking out of rage, but she made a mistake right away. Sometimes it seemed as though her mother damaged her ego. "I was only trying to help you," she said. Her dad stands up and intervenes on their behalf. Everyone remained perplexed about what to do. "Enough, Manya, go to your room."

Manya also raised her voice, saying, "Wow, it's me again; you don't say anything to her; actually, you should be an actor because no one can catch you." However, her father becomes agitated and tugs her hand, confining her to her room. Danish sprint to thwart him. "Refrain from opening the door."

"It's my fault; I ought to leave."

"Indeed, you ought to," he remarked, making no attempt to impede them. More drama is not what he wants. Ritwik couldn't say more than glance around before they departed.

❧❧❧

Chapati was beginning to dry out. Danish put a plate over it. He waited for Manya to open the door still. He is aware of her tendency to forget things quickly, but when she becomes irate, she stops talking and eating. Even though he kept pounding on the door, she remained silent. He said, "I am still waiting when you open the door," as he reached out to her. Her voice broke, "Go home; I have enough; I don't need food." She continued to cry. He was unsure about what to do.

The door opened abruptly, and she kicked him. He felt a little drowsy. Pulling her leg, he said, "What I did now." he stumbles a bit. "Nothing, you're just bothersome," she remarked while taking the plate and setting it down in the kitchen. She returns to her room. However, she didn't lock this time.

"I'm tired of being average," he muttered, coming into the room and sitting on the floor where she was lying. She gave him a quick glance without saying anything. Bring up their unresolved fight with him. He continues to get no response when he says, "At least turn on your phone." Danish was starting to nod off once more. Within a single breath, she seemed to be trying to tell someone, "You saw there he defended her like I was wrong, how I'm always wrong, she didn't even come when I met with an accident, she is the one who doesn't want me, she never calls, and suddenly she wants that I remember her and take her help, why do that, when I will have my own life." She gets up and Danish adds, "It's your birthday; at least eat something and then talk." She's glaring at him once more. "I'd prefer not to eat."

She still sob there on the floor. It's not just that moment it rewind all the mishaps of life. she put her head on his shoulder,

closed eyes, drooling down tear. He gently brushes her hair in a room of silence.

Manya didn't say anything for three days, but she appeared fine. Not that she went outside to eat. Danish made her eat, so she did in the end. She didn't use social media, so she didn't even use it for 5 days. She kept the phone off and didn't post anything. She stays silent while sitting in her room.

"Sorry, Manya. Would you please just stop right now?" Her father was waiting for her at the door, hoping she would open it. He held off. She emerged a few minutes later. She had a bag and was prepared for college. She turned to go after saying, "I apologize for overreacting," but he stopped her. He gave the tiffin to her. She hoped he would say something, but he remained silent. Upon accepting the tiffin, she remained motionless.

"Would you like to say anything?"

"I would like to, but it appears that you are unwilling to listen."

"Say, I'm standing here."

"I cannot deny you that your mother can file a case against me, and despite what she said, she was attempting to assist you. I did not invite her beforehand. She may be using a complex vocabulary, and you may have been impolite to her. That will only serve to set you apart even more. I'm trying, but I have no idea what kind of connection we will have in the future. I understand that you have had challenges throughout your life, but I went through hardships too, and I don't want you to continue going through it. I understand you don't talk about it with me, but it's crucial," he uttered, his voice breaking as he revealed his difficulties. He had every image that showed how the two of them formed a father and daughter family. Manya appears astonished that she occasionally overlooks her father. "I apologize; I suppose I can be selfish occasionally. I hope I don't disappoint you in the future, but I can't promise you about mum." She wants to give him a hug, but she always feels uncomfortable becoming emotional with her dad. She displayed her feelings in front of him; perhaps she inherited them from him.

They parted ways without exchanging hugs and continued. But Manya pulled over at the side of the road and sat quietly on the bench. Always lost in her own thoughts, she never pays attention to anyone else. She don't even grumble about her father, Danish, and his family—she just causes trouble for other people. They also make a constant effort to lift her spirits. That Danish guy kept coming over to see if she was eating. Make every effort to persuade her not to fight. Her father has been living alone for a long time, and he finds it just as tough to live alone as it is to live without a mother. Although he has never expressed his loneliness to her in his entire life, that doesn't imply he doesn't. She understands that although seeing her mother hurts her, her father is pained more. While Mom has moved on and lived her own life, he continues to work at the same company without the ideal family that everyone aspires to.

The more she considered it, the heavier she felt. Not sorry wasn't going to address the issue in a fair manner. She removed her phone from the purse. She turned on. She received a notification on her phone. Checking her social media accounts. That was not the case. She looked through her email and saw that she got a call and other texts from Danish. Subsequently, she noticed that Kartik had also sent her multiple messages.

"Do you feel alright?"

"Are you occupied?, you did not attend college."

"What transpires? Are things going well?"

"Are you coming on the festival day tomorrow?"

Numerous messages were present. While messaging him, she showed no ego, but Manya was so furious that she ignored everything else. She is merely wasting this ability that she have. She felt sorry for him; he must be wondering where she had gone. He must be anticipating her response. She has since expanded her list of contacts. She observes individuals going about their daily lives. She fled because she thought that everyone should accept responsibility. She believed she ought to be grateful to everyone. She was unable to get Kartik off her mind.

"Should I respond to him today?" She was prepared to date Kartik, but she is afraid that all of her decisions will be rejected. She cannot, however, reject the existence of life. People captivate you. Additionally, you may always assume the worst.

"I apologize for not being able to get in touch with you. I had a problem." She conceals a lot of things in whatever she says, "I'll meet you and tell you everything." She tried to fix her problem right away, feeling a little relieved that she was acting like an adult. He answered right away.

"I'm waiting"

She doesn't know that what she is doing. Is it right?. But she want to take action. She don't want her life to be like she scare to have.

❧❧❧

"What made you vanish, or were you abducted this time?" There, Shresth felt unnoticed. Manya was astounded to learn how much she had missed during her brief retreat from society. The college doesn't look as it does usually. Banners were used to decorate it completely. The most attractive item she saw was a food truck, which she ignored. From the crowd emerged Niti. Her goal was successfully completed.

With a coffee came. She said, "Nobody present this much, but for fest, huh." She becomes aware of Manya's survival. "I had a fight at home," she admitted, aware that she would soon be interrogated. Because they didn't want to get in the way of her family, they didn't ask any more questions. They observed theatrical productions from many sections as they peered around. Manya is a little bummed about it because she had hoped to demonstrate her Kathak dances. Everyone's attention was drawn to a stall where food and handcrafted goods might be sold. Niti was partial to a long Indian earring, but because they weren't haggling, she passed it up.

"How is Kartik doing? He is not returning the call." Manya is attempting to contact him still.

"He went with Yash, so I saw him but I didn't get to meet him," Shresth said, startled that Yash and he had become friends. We come to a conclusion at the stage area. A girl trio was dancing in a hip-hop fashion before switching to Bollywood, to the delight of all those there. Manya was too busy looking for Kartik to be having fun. She called him again. Didn't reply. To dance, Shresth took her hand. She took a few steps. The music ends.

"Karthik is here," yelled Shresth. Everybody faces the stage. He held the microphone. Manya and Kartik locked gaze. Everyone was yelling for the music to resume. "I apologize for disturbing you all." Everyone fell silent, as he felt compelled to speak. "I want to apologize to someone because I was unable to pay attention to you."

"Apologies," exclaimed Shresth.

"I truly love you, and I want to love forever. Please pardon me, Mansi."

All of them hutting. Manya was taken aback. Her lips dropped open in shock. Yash whisper from her shoulder to his chin as he approached from behind. He chuckles, "His love changes, mine doesn't." By pushing him. As Kartik descended, everyone applauded him. Though Mansi approached from behind, Kartik proceeded to give her a hug the moment she got to him. Manya, a single woman who was going to transform her life, witnessed all of this, yet...

CHAPTER ELEVEN

"Where are you trying to look?" Manya is awakened by a Danish's mother. She didn't know his mother was calling her because she was staring so intently. Though she was in the kitchen, Manya was in her line of sight. She was concerned about her expression. Perhaps it was because she would be alone after Danish left, she reasoned. She didn't cut her off. Abruptly, she stands up and begins to assist. It was unusual for her to be silent. The plate she was scrubbing was clean. She was doing it once more now. She remarked, "That's enough cleaning," and picked up every plate.

Once more, Manya was not seated at the supper table with them. She enjoys having dinner and watching a performance. Normally, Danish participates, but he doesn't want to miss spending time with his seniors. Everyone knows she's not quite right. Nonetheless, they fear a new confrontation. Delicate Manya. "What do you have to eat?" Danish sat next to her and said, "Your plate is empty." He met her side eyes with his own. Her gaze was fixed on the television. "What is the tale?" Her own realization dawned on her that she was merely observing. She doesn't know much about the series, but she has to respond to him. Knowing she wasn't even trying to look smarter, he nodded. Knowing something was about to come up, he smiled and looked sideways as he said, "And what your story." She turned to face him like a puppy, debating whether or not to tell him. However, she is genuinely eager to share it with someone. He turns her face toward the TV and adds, "If you don't want to tell me, just don't, but don't make that face; it's making me...". Yeah he was blushing.

She muttered, "That's why I wasn't telling; now it feels strange to tell you these things." Knowing she would speak up in some way, he remained silent. "All right, so you are aware that I turned off my phone and didn't respond to anyone for a number of days; in reality, Kartik asked me to go on a date right away." She said something that the Danish clearly didn't like. Nevertheless, he holds back out of a desire to keep her life unhindered. "Well, I gave it some thought and maybe I should be with someone." Breathing seemed to be beyond his reach. "Alright, that's fresh."

"Yes, that's correct, but I thought I had spoken to him today, and then I noticed there was a festival at campus. Alright, everything was going well, everyone was dancing, and then all of a sudden he approached the stage, expressed regret, and admitted that Mansi was her lover's interest—whatever that meant!". Although she was clenching up, Danish looked away. "That's the reason I kept it from you."

"Do you know if he accepts it? He didn't accept it, so that doesn't mean you like him. You like him. That's not my win." He started to become a little serious and confused at the same time. Though he tried to keep them hidden, his true emotions were becoming apparent.

She felt bad and said, "I am sorry, I am hurting you. I will tell you later." Like after it wouldn't hurt.

"It's okay, you mentioned that it takes courage as well; nothing happen sad for you," he says as he stands up and takes her plate.

❧❧❧

Manya experienced some discomfort. It occurs to her that she slept on the couch. She was in the Danish house when she opened her eyes. And yet she was so tired. For her, sadness became the dominant emotion. She curled up inside the blanket because it was cold outside. She is unwilling to stand up. Sound asleep again. Danish knew that she was dozing off on the couch. He emerged to make sure. Upon noticing that the AC conditioning was insufficient, he increased it. He just stood there, giving her a quick glance. She awakens. "It was excessively chilly," he said while gesturing to the remote. Before long, they become awkward. Danish quickly returns to his room.

....

Take a stance. "Manya is arriving," Yash said in the foyer, capturing everyone's interest. She felt ashamed. Her face was hidden. "Don't you have any enemies but me," she hurriedly remarked. Her pursued him. He laughs, "You are my beloved woman."

She moved in the direction of the auditorium. The exercise has started. They both remained motionless, biding their time. "Well, may I ask you a serious question? Will you be here tomorrow? Dressed in a saree," he says. She thought is it really serious. The play was presented in the era of India's freedom. She said, "I don't know, I want to go, but my life," with no greater clarity. The teacher is all around her, and she is reluctant to swear. Manya in costume was nothing like her real one. She had a pallu on her head and was dressed in a basic cotton saree.

As she was walking by, a student said, "You look weird, Manya."

"Hey you," Yash was unable to respond. He called out, but he was nowhere to be seen.

"You are not the only one who is blind; it was a joke."

He perceived it as either recognition or slight.

They both turn to face the stage. "I'll come get you tomorrow." "No, thank you." Chatting along, even up on stage. "Is there anything more crucial, Manya and Yash?" The instructor yelled at them. "No," they nodded.

"Are you coming tomorrow"

"Oh yes" still started chatting.

"Simply don't create any issues; that's all," Manya's father consented to her visiting Lonavala. And she consented to let Yash accompany her. Shresth and Niti were going to accompany. She was a little intrigued about him, but she let it go. She was not sure about Kartik. Only two days were spent on the brief excursion. She is not heavy. She doesn't travel too far most of the time. Yash was waiting for her in the vehicle. She realizes he has been honking for a long and dashes outside. When she notices he's left a seat next to him, she slows down. She knew he had done it already. She appears excited, as does everyone else. Niti and Shresth applaud her. "Manya, Manya." Yash joins "My lovely Manya" as well.

He teases her, saying, "Kartik already reached the toll, and we are here because you are late."

"Have I enquired about him?" She actually remarked, "You have so many problems; okay, I will stay at home," as she opened the door. Still, he grasps her hand. Everyone laughs and says, "I am going just for you." Save for Manya. "Dumb flirting"

As they started driving. A passenger in the back slept. She cautioned Yash, saying, "A minute ago, they were so excited; now they are sleeping; you don't sleep." He cranked up the tunes, to alter one's emotions. He meant it when he said, "You can sleep." But she didn't; the driver will get tired too if no one spoke to him. "No, I can drive if you get sleepy."

Yash used the music system to call Kartik. A part of Manya hoped he hadn't picked up. But he immediately got the hang of it. He exclaimed, sounding pleased, "You are so late." Manya stops him with a punch, saying, "It's not me." Although he didn't like it, he can tolerate anything because it was Manya. "I'll get closer soon." His laughter was loud. When Shresth awoke, he saw Yash as usual, but he had gone back to sleep.

He halted the vehicle abruptly. He bellowed, "Tea break." "Don't you think we should be taking a break sooner?" Niti is unwilling to leave. She wishes to connect with everyone there. "No rush, we're here to chill." Shresth did concur. Since Manya wasn't feeling well, she stated she would do anything as long as she could only agree to accompany them, which is exactly what she was doing. Yash gave her the chai cup as they strolled along.

People are crossing the road where they are standing. "You are upset that a guy rejected you because you haven't responded in a few days, and he didn't inquire as to why; he moved on to another girl." Shresth merely gazed at him. Here we go once more. "I understand, Scenario you don't have to explain everything to me over and over again," she uttered as she threw the mud cup like a basketball from a distance. And she did it well. But Yash was anxious for the real deal. Yash was surprised by Manya's statement, "I think he was just confused; I also didn't respond for many days." Manya was the one who occasionally utilized reasoning in her conversations. Listening to them from behind was Shresth. Her mood was known to him. "She will taste betrayal and realize it," Shresth kidded. They hurry over to the car. "Leave; love literally drives people crazy."

❦❦❦

Niti gave her a head pat to rouse her. "Look at your traitor," she gestured. Together with Mansi in tow

"What?" Yash exclaimed loudly.

"Gently," she said.

"Well, I forgot Manya has too many men," she replied, tugging at her cheeks.

"I am here to enjoy it; forget it," she said, fastening her seatbelt.

Shresth gathered every bag from the rear. "Where is my bag?" Standing there, Manya realizes that perhaps she left her bag at home. Inside the car, everyone checks. Manya was taken aback by her extreme sadness at forgetting the luggage. She continued to be cool and remarked, "Everyone, let's accept that I mess up again. The car is not on 4 acres that we cannot see." Manya looks at Yash and says, "Actually, I accept when you start finding the bag."

After deciding to purchase a room, everyone considers the abundance of clothing. Manya walked slowly. Because she isn't ready to speak with Kartik. To escape the outside world, she pulls out her phone. Danish had ten missed calls, she saw. Little Gulp predicted that he would act strangely around her. He could have said, "Hey, you forgot your bag at home," but instead he just grumbled. She said, fearing his lecture, "Sorry, I didn't pick; I slept soundly; don't bother; I will buy some clothes here." He hung up without saying anything.

While the rooms were being prepared, the entire class sat in the garden area and enjoyed the refreshments. When Manya looked at Kartik and Mansi, Yash stated, "She said forget it, but I don't see that coming from her." Together, Niti and Shresth respond, "Yeah, I can see." They were mad at her.

"Hey" the fear of interaction went away when everyone arrived. Manya was certain he would visit them. "We arrived in an hour; you were busy," Yash and Kartik grew close to one another. Yash enveloped his shoulder with his hand. They no longer growl at one another. It wasn't necessary to add, "Manya forgot her bag," but Shresth felt compelled to. Manya was mortified. "Then what?" She rolled her eyes and remarked, "I can get the clothes." Grabbing the keys from Yash, she dragged Niti inside the room with her.

Niti looked elegant when she went to supper with everyone. And Manya remained in bed, just as she had been in the morning. Not even face wash might help shift things. She wants food, though, so she doesn't care right now. The door rang. Manya opened the door, saw that someone was outside, and shut it. Upon opening the door once more, she realized she had forgotten the bag. "I saw it there. I was certain it would be Danish." Chasing after him, she ran. He moved quickly; he nearly reached his car. From the rear she plucked him , she took up his T-shirt. He turned to face her and yelled, "Oh god, you can do other things, but you chose this," but then he burst out laughing. She opened her eyes. She took a look at her own phone. She was pleased with herself and said, "I know I should comb my hair, but it's not that bad."

"I felt that I should be thanked." As she pulled in the direction of the hotel, she exclaimed, "Danish, you are my eternal saviour."

He walked over to the car and said, "I have to go home."

"It's late, and I really appreciated it, I have a lot of justifications," she repeated.

"Your friends become uncomfortable," he interrupts.

"They won't feel uncomfortable; you will." That's accurate.

He was compelled to concur with her even more. "But now that you're without clothes," she abruptly interrupts him as he is pulling. "Actually, I have; I was going to stay, but not where everyone will be, and I thought to go back the next day," she begins tugging once more. "I get around on foot"

A large number of people approach the eatery directly. Danish stops when he realizes this. It was packed, and he repeated inaudibly, "You wanted change." She repeated, "No, just come in; I look fine." But break free from her bonds. "You look amazing all the time," he replied, sounding smug.

"Danish," Yash said when he first saw him. She drew him to sit next to her and said, "He came here to give my bag, so I requested that he stay." She is aware of his social awkwardness around a lot of people. "Why are there so many people in this place?" Danish whispers in her ears. But she paid him no mind. "Manya, what happened to you?" Kartik makes fun of her. "Don't you know that I am a self-exclaim beauty?" she replied, rolling her eyes and folding her hand. "My vote counts," declares Danish as he raises his glass in unison with everyone else. "Observe my army," she cried out.

Kartik Said, "You can share a room with me, Danish." That caught everyone off guard. Throw tissues at Kartik; "I thought you and Mansi. Share room," Yash was unable to finish because of Kartik. He answered, "You don't have to worry; I have to go tomorrow. I have to be prepared because I have a flight on Saturday of next week." He only wanted to inform one person about this, though. He informed her, and she was astonished, but she didn't realize they would have time to spend together before he left. However, she simply forgets in her arguments with her father, her love betrayed, and her travels with friends.

"Therefore, you ought to remain," Shresth declared

Danish looked down and stated, "I don't want to jump in this because I don't hate my life." When he mentioned he has extreme fears, he wasn't lying. However, everyone shuddered from the high. Interestingly, Manya had self-doubt as well. No one was preparing; they were just pushing each other to jump. She retreated, yelled, clutched his hands, and they dove into the water together. She kept saying, "Danish, see, see this," as she tried to make him see underwater, but he struggled due to the abrupt jump. "I don't see anything, why me?" he exclaims, stepping away. "I won't let Grandpa go with us the next time," Manya said, struggling to open her eyes underwater. As he observed everyone, his thoughts shifted. He was uncomfortable among everyone, even if he wasn't displaying it. He was always behind Manya, like a child. She'll take care of everything. A few approached him, but he was at a loss for words.

"Danish, please come here," yelled a girl. Manya shoves him. He took a step back. He lamented being able to act as though he hadn't heard. However, it was him who responded with haste. Actually, he sighed. He had no desire to venture outside of the secure haven. Manya was starting to feel at ease and thought that it wasn't all that horrible. Knowing that Danish was out there, she considered pursuing him.

Not that good around other people. She remarked, "You took a lot of time." Danish thought, "Is she crazy? I'm not sure," she notices that.

The water frightened him. He chuckled uneasily and said, "Yeah, actually, we are in water." Manya was drifting there like a fish. Simply view them. "You don't know who I am; my name is Saumya." Danish considered telling her his name, but she was already aware of it. He made his introduction earlier. He was waiting on a response from her, but all she could do was smile and look at him. "I thought you wanted to say something," he said, not very amused. It's a little annoying of her. She doesn't stop, though. "Would you like to go on the boat with us?" With grace, she inquired.

"Yes, exactly—why not?" Manya appears and responds on his behalf. By pushing him.

Because he was tired of it, he didn't dispute it this time. "Yes, it's fine." Manya appeared pleased that he was forming friendships there. She gave him a contented mother's watch. She tucked herself in. On the rock, and sat. It was in the twilight. It appears like the relaxing holiday is proceeding smoothly. "What brings you here? Did you fail to board the boat?" Kartik returned from behind.

"I simply want to spend some time by myself," she remarked as she took a sip of her beer. Turning, he peered in Mansi's direction. In the café, everyone else seemed to be enjoying themselves. Next to her, Kartik took a seat. She glanced at her as well.

She folds her lips and murmurs, "Oh, she is beautiful and soft spoken."

He smirks and says, "Stop saying things when you don't mean them."

She moaned, "Yeah, she's so annoyed."

"To put it mildly, not that much."

"I'm sorry, okay."

She enjoys making messes a lot. He questioned when she would completely shut her mouth and cease saying things so incredibly dumb. He couldn't tell if she was just acting like that or if her communication abilities were actually lacking. But it slipped her mind. She is less awkward than Kartik. Manya is considering the reasons he might have visited her. "What brings you here?" She reasoned that it would be best to ask him personally. He put her straight by posing a question. With a smile on his face, he assumed she would never change. "I came because I saw you alone," he laugh uncontrollably. She simply grinned and nodded. We looked at each other, and they remained silent. But a lot was being said with their eyes. She abruptly turned her face and said, "I just learned this a few days ago; I am very stubborn, and you have an ego and are also impatient."

There was a Danish voice, "I am going." Manya comes to the realization that he is over socializing. She got up to follow him. "Where're you heading?" Danish had no desire to respond. He merely gave her a quick glance before returning to the hotel. Yet again, Manya acted without thinking. She was experiencing all that she said and did.

"It's time for you to leave; that obnoxious woman is gazing at me."

"Hello!"

Manya didn't know what the Danish room number was. "I can try, and I'll apologize right away." Her decision. She thought 301. After knocking once, she discovered they had a bell. She just made one press. No one was answering. Her attempt to hear his voice was beginning. She made numerous calls. "Are you blind, don't you see disturb sign?" The man did not sound Danish when he shouted she quickly guess. Confirmed that it was other room. "I was close, it was 302, and I guess I'm impatient too." Her error had horrified her. She offers the man her apology. Danish opened the door for her, but they didn't seem to be in the mood for a talk. Manya came in and settled herself erect on the bed; she was truly exhausted from swimming. She irritates him since she is hungry, but she decides to speak with Danish first. Once more, however, words were not action.

"Why are you going at night, may I ask?" He had been packing. Lacking any interest in anything. Not even that he was glancing at her. There, she sighed. She gets up and stands behind him. "Okay, I won't push you to go with other people; I am sorry," she says. "Do you truly want to know or is this just something else?". Manya was unable to speak. She is aware that more should be done to incite his rage. "You actually don't know that I'm leaving; when people leave, they normally go crazy, but I'm planning on spending some time with everyone. I assumed that when I arrived, I would be with you, and after that, we would be alone, but you don't seem to care; in fact, you seem to have forgotten that I am leaving."

"I sincerely apologize; I didn't realize."

His tears rarely happened, but they were there as he said, "I am not asking for too much just as a friend; I don't want to fight with you, but you never understand nor my feelings now, not even my friendship, that's the." She understood that saying sorry would not help. Others are harmed by her immature behave. "I truly apologize, and I mean it. I always make mistakes, but for now, all I can do is attempt to find a solution." She truly said, "I will be with you till you go, and I will make sure you are happy." He was reluctant to speak.

Manya made sure she would always be with him, even though she managed to persuade him to come and enjoy everyone. She is fortunate to have her friendship with him, even though she is unaware of it, because he did not act out against her. He was still not spending much time with her. Both felt comfortable. "We have a game planned. I've created a variety of difficulties, such as having to sprint first, touch a rod, eat six hot pani puris, solve a problem, then return to the starting point. Although it appears simple, there is a chance that you will be stopped by someone. The victor will receive two cups of instant noodles, but the pretender will be eliminated." Instant Noodle comments ranged from high to low, but the game was still engaging. Everyone is paired off, and sadly, Saumya is paired with a Danish. "I'm going to play with Danish." She is desperate because she feels like everyone is staring at her. "I can guide him; he's fragile and doesn't play usually." Although Saumya didn't like the idea, Manya moved with Danish because she didn't want to keep making the same mistakes.

"Leave now." Manya was more ecstatic. "You find this game so easy," Danish at last remarked. She was happy at once. "Yes, I can be annoying at any time." Danish begins running, but Manya clutches his leg. Everyone copied her after they saw her. One side of her was heavy. He was a pretty good drag. Manya found amazing pani puri challenging since she wanted some too. She attempted to stop him from eating when she detected it, but he moved quickly. The hardest puzzle was the last one. It was such a simple problem, but Manya was relaxed and easily botched it when he ordered she trash them all. They were having difficulty, but they laughed a lot. They acknowledge that they were defeated. Shresth outpaces them in speed. "Oh, I wanted the cup of noodles," Manya stumbled to the floor in exhaustion. "Who said I should be so committed to you stops me?" They had fun even though they were unable to win.

It's Saumya and Shresth who triumph. Suddenly, Manya appeared, took the Shresth rewards, and fled. He went after her. "To be honest, this doesn't even make sense."

❧❧❧

"What made us arrive so early?" At the airport, Manya was unable to locate a seat. Standing, her feet went numb. Resting on one of the Danish suitcases was her. His three large bags. Though his family simply wants him to see more and more, he could depart. And Manya's father came; he typically did not come from his assignment, but he did come. Everything an Asian is taught by their parents is what his family tells him. They even talk about his marriage. They had witnessed his entire life at the airport in a split second. Manya was also upset, but she pretended not to be, so everyone could relax. Her father is also a huge Danish fan, albeit he keeps it to himself. Danish put on the watch he brought right away. Manya felt so good about surprise by father.

It was a really good promise kept by Manya. After graduation, she was a huge help to him; she would come help with packing and make sure he didn't forget anything. She gave him a lot of gifts. She understood she would be alone now, unlike when they used to pack together. She has now learned how to truly live her father's life from him. She looks at each person slowly. What they do, and they conceal it.

His mother held up while his Danish father sobbed and gave him a hug. She tried to defuse the situation by saying, "Let's check again 100 times your passport and ticket everything is right," but she was powerless. Danish eyes were moist as well. He gave Manya a quick hug. They arrived on time, but he wasn't. He's going to be late. Because of long goodbye. Manya grinned. All they said to one another was "be careful." He gave an embrace. So he hurried to the airport. Everybody is outdoors, observing waiting for him to get his tickets.

Manya understands the feeling she gets when she lets others in. It is both new and depressing. However, she is only able to sense pain there. Watching people leave as she stood there. Although they can return and depart, relationships grow incredibly strained. The thing that scared her the most was that leaving things behind.

CHAPTER TWELVE

Four years later

"It's like a pill to us, therefore let's call our stunning actress who has done so many films in such a short amount of time and so many hilarious reality shows. Ladies and gentlemen, I would like to give her a call and inform her more about her character, welcome Manya Singh. The journalists and spectators were crammed into the mall. Manya was positioned next to the platform. She entered the stage. She took the stage as the first performer in the cast to do so. "Hello, I am Manya thanks to all of you coming here. I appreciate everyone's presence here."

"You're portraying the lead role, sister; how's that going?". With a short glance at the ubiquitous poster, Manya turned. She was only a sidekick, but it seemed huge and magnificent from where she was standing. Even yet, she was glad to get to work and sighed. They arrived late, but the other actor did as well. Manya simply arrived first to fill in the empty space. She stepped aside. No one treats her rudely. Even yet, she wasn't the primary character and didn't receive the same attention as others. But sometime people treat differently.

She still has the unflappable smile after four years. Over the years, she has been involved in everything. Manya lacks a plan. She takes on whatever opportunity that presents itself, whether it's a minor part in a movie or an advertisement. She has done so many movies for this reason that she can't even recall ever landing a little part—five minutes is plenty for her.

Despite her intense dedication to her job, she has not received the respect she deserves. In actuality, her comedy were the most well-liked across the nation. These shows usually go out of style, but Manya brought them back into style. She still prefers to work on motion pictures than reality TV. At times, you have to act in order to make money. She pledged not to accept her father's money. She moved from the house to a modest, cosy, but expensive, apartment for this reason. She purchased an car for herself as a result of her career in show industry. She once left the airport on foot. The paparazzi arrived, naturally, to photograph another actor, although they did manage to catch a glimpse of her. Manya discovers she doesn't have an car when she abruptly stops. She now regrets renting a car the following day. It is not at all helpful. She decided that appearing impoverished was preferable. It's difficult to be independent. Still, she brought on Sanvi as a manager. She was more of a friend, but it hurts that you have to pay her since she is an employee of yours.

Through some means, Sanvi said, "Hey Manya, it's done; come done." Manya lost their position and didn't receive a lot of advancement timing. "Yes, I will be there." They both headed straight for the parking area. Although she wasn't very well-known, she still has followers. Sanvi took the chocolate that Manya had taken out of her bag and gave to herself right away. "You promised to follow a diet."

"What's the purpose?"

Inside the parking lot, there was calm. They were unwilling to go. It has been a long few days of heavy effort for them. They are in dire need of a getaway. Manya won't permit that to occur. Since reality shows are typically filmed in various locations, even while the cast is on holiday, they are still working there. Everybody's heads are heavy. Sanvi added, "Now we have a go party," as she pulled open her phone to see the itinerary. "Who throws a party at midday?" Manya sighed. Indians typically enjoy evening parties. Morning or noon, it makes no difference to them. She cannot dispute the fact that she must leave, though. "It's a dance party with cocktails," Sanvi declared. At midday, they both wonder who feels like dancing. Sanvi chose the spot to minimize traffic. "Should I put on new clothes?" disapproved of her blue dress. She tries to dress more maturely, but traffic prevents her from making the shift.

Sanvi remarked, "It's again, Mansi; I heard this movie has such a high budget," as she noticed the large billboard poster. Manya simply gazed at it. She no longer feels jealous now that she is an adult, but her Manya to succeed still there. However, nothing is happening as planned. The lack of excitement in the films that were given makes her sad these days. "Don't worry, Niti will be there." It gave her a small sense of relief.

Manya went to find Niti right away; her daughter was sobbing. She was humming various jingles to herself to fall asleep. Manya began to sing along as well. After some time, she had fallen asleep. Manya smirks, "Your daughter shouts like you." All Niti did was nod. Niti is unavoidable; get up and grab Manya a drink. She understands that she must leave her bed. "Who is that woman from abroad? Never have I seen her." Numerous people glances at her due to her stunning beauty. She was fascinated by her appearance. "It's Yash's girlfriend," she said. Manya receives a shock. A girl falls in love with an annoying guy. "She is working on a movie under his production, and then you know," says Niti, who is well-versed in business rumours. Niti was an actor, and among those who received the greatest feedback from the public and business community was her. Her first movie became an Ionic, but she wasn't making movies the day she made the decision to be married. She enjoyed her time working in the field.

"I am amazed at Kartik's ability to take Shresth as the main lead in his film, but he never showed any of us his work personally. Kartik, I don't know what he is doing, girl, he gets so easily," Niti said, looking at Kartik. Solitary in the throng. A few years later, he stopped talking. Once upon a time, he was the life of the party. He now projects an air of intellectual individuality in his presentation. "Stop staring at him; he knows who we are." They both avert their eyes.

"Hey ladies, how's your baby doing?" Shresth turned to face the pram her daughter was riding in. How he loves her. His look has undergone significant alteration. Now he was better groomed. In actuality, everyone modifies their looks in some way to appear visually appealing to the audience. Everybody aspires to have their unique look. "Manya, I always watch your Himachal video while I eat dinner; I watch it so much." He meant it sincerely. His compliments make Manya feel good. Of course, compliments are nice to receive. Manya adores it.

"I got a call, Manya. Another reality program exists, but what's the deal? in the United States." Sanvi ran over, her excitement surpassing Manya's. Although she appreciated the comment, she is not motivated to pursue further endeavours. However, she never did in the US, and that truly occurred to her. Manya is unsure about what to do about it and says, "But I don't want to." But it might be enjoyable, she thought. "Why do you not want to?" They all adore it. Shresth wasn't prepared for this response.

"I want to make movies, that's why"

"At the very least, you two can take a vacation," Niti attempts to persuade her.

"Yeah, take a vacation with her to unwind with that I have to take another." Although Sanvi is worn out, she still wants to take part in this. Manya was becoming receptive to it. Being idle is preferable to working.

"Let's simply meet them, alright".

"This bag contains what?" Manya shuddered, carrying the bulky luggage up the stairs. Using the suitcase he had purchased for her, his father assisted her. "What matters is what you don't have in your house." Even though Manya was on the second story, it seemed like ten. She put the bag down and inhaled deeply. "Give me the key," he thought to himself as he opened the gate. because it appears as though she will pass out from mere movement. As she approached the front door, Manya declared, "There is no need for a key." Furthermore, the lock was simple to open when she kicked it. She set the lock aside. Her father was stunned by what had transpired and was standing there. "Is one lock not enough for you?"

"Don't worry, there's nothing to steal."

Although a tad crowded, her apartment is adorable. Dirt, though, was all over. She cleans it, but nothing changes. They walked to the kitchen together to prepare coffee and read the script for Manya's upcoming movie. There are moments when he can be her expert. Manya kept interrupting him as he was reading the script. "In a few days, I'll be in the US."

"Oh, I see. I should give that to Danish. I'll give it to you later." He was enumerating the items he want to gift. Manya realized that, at the time of her employment, she had not given Danish any thought. It's not like they don't get along. They do not often speak on the phone. They're both awkward and busy. He was right about everything; he will begin a new life. Then then, they call each other on their birthday.

They still have the same voices and tone of voice, but they are now discussing various vocations. Everyone was pleased to see that he was employed by a reputable company and had a solid track record. Danish initially found it difficult to be honest with others, but he persisted and did his best on his own. At first, they spoke on the phone a lot, but as time went on, there was a gradual decrease in the frequency of phone calls from both parties. However, Danish did not forget to watch her movie and text the review over the phone.

He added, "I'm going to video call Danish; come here," having the sudden thought that he ought to speak with Danish but not reveal Manya's whereabouts. He thought up the plan to surprise him. He seemed happier than Manya. It didn't mean that Manya no longer liked him, but they had established a barrier that neither of them can cross. Manya used to check to make sure she didn't appear awful in the mirror. The speed with which he picked it up was astounding.

"Hello, this is where it's morning," he adds, pointing out his office's outside.

"Hey," she replies abruptly and courteously, recalling how she used to yell at him. Upon seeing her after all this time, Danish was in awe. "How are you doing?" Danish inquired straight away after noticing a strange location in the back. "This is my rented apartment; I moved in here because I have work and I come late." In actuality, Manya keeps this from him. She didn't want to inform him about this because she didn't know herself. "Your apartment is adorable," he remarked, and she felt happy that she had at least done some cleaning. To speak with him, Manya's father picked up the phone. He always discusses everything with him. Are you bothered by anyone? Are you having any problems? Are things going well there? His transformation is quite endearing. He shows everyone how meticulous he is.

Manya made the decision that he would be better off getting married in the past. He would be delighted to have someone share his life. He doesn't seem to have found anyone. It would be foolish of her to decide to marry him off on her own. The day he wanted to come, she waited for him, but he never showed up. She is in awe of anyone who can live alone. Next, she is acting on her own.

Danish had to go, he had work. However, it caused Manya to have a happy-looking smile on her face. She's always delighted about it.

He heard Manya's voice as Danish was eating a sandwich. He turned to see his friend watching his reality show, the renowned one about Himachal Pradesh. He also peeps in to see from a distance. He noticed that his co-worker was having a great time with the show.

"Oh my, you really saw her show," an acerbic guy approached.

He finds it amusing that "Given our distance from the city, being in nature seems somewhat rejuvenating." The Danish are extremely proud of it.

He remarked, "Funny, I think she's cringy," which surprised the Danish. However, he didn't like what he said, and everyone has different viewpoints. He retreated, as though oblivious to the events taking place, yet he was listening to their quarrel.

"Danish, how do you feel about her content? You are Indian, thus you must have seen her." Danish struggled to come up with a response for them. Their glistening eyes were waiting to see how he would respond. But even though they don't communicate often, he didn't want to disparage her closest buddy. He still holds her in high regard.

"I didn't watch any of her shows, in fact. But I think she is good." The greatest way out he could find

"Oh, I didn't realize you had to watch it." He felt a little let down.

"Hey, who's that?" After her father left, Manya went to sleep. She skipped dinner entirely. She was so exhausted that she dozed off immediately. She didn't get dressed differently. An annoyance called her in the middle of the night. "How can you forget me every time? I have to remind you over and over." Manya becomes aware that she is in a relationship. She occasionally forgets. She doesn't even consider calling him if he doesn't. Everyone describes her behaviour toward everyone in this way. She is devoid of love and affection. She is aware of his existence, but the issue lies in her tendency to disregard her responsibilities. She abruptly woke up. She said courteously, "I was busy the whole day; I couldn't call you," after coming to the startling conclusion. He signs, "You would have to call me if you cared. I am the same as you, and I work every day."

Actor Rohit was another. He and she met. It was all quite normal when they were filming a movie together, but their love was not normal. For a month, Manya was smitten with him, but she swiftly lost interest, as is evident to all. The audience is still enamoured with their relationship. However, it is Manya who has entered the incorrect formula into this chemical. Rohit wanted to try not to hurt Manya's heart, even if Manya did admit that they should part ways. But Rohit never agree to it, and she goes back to putting up with it. Manya just wants it to stop so she can go back to sleep; she doesn't have a response. She said, "I'm sorry, I just can't help myself," hoping that would persuade him. "Thank you very much! I'm sorry, but it's your 30th sorry." He remarked, startled to realize he had been counting. He was furious. Even though he was constantly preaching, Manya fell asleep.

"Rohit, please take another look at the one I told you earlier." Manya was conscious.

"What?"

She yelled, "That I want to sleep, and I don't want to be with you."

"Whoa, you want to split up because you want to go to bed. That's okay, I respect myself." She broke off in the middle.

"Thank you so much more than you had before, mwah," she threw her aside and exclaimed.

Danish return home by car. A breeze filled the air, he felt. All he wants to eat is something warm. And shortly return home. When he came home, he changed right away. He usually does the dishes first, but he skipped because he was being slick. In search of something to eat, he headed to the kitchen. He opened his refrigerator to find leftover breakfast and then looked for Manya's reality show on television. It displayed a lot of results, and he assumed he had seen a lot. He's seen every episode so many times that he was at a loss for what to watch again. He consumes the remaining food in the meanwhile. He made instant noodles since he was hungry. And back on the couch once more. Her shows paired perfectly with Noodle. He found the sensation to be soothing.

After Noodle was done, he continued to watch and chuckle despite being aware of the joke. Ring came on. "Arriving." First, he looked at the security monitor. He was instantly thrilled to see his fiancée. He pulled open the door right away. He embraced her.

"Why did you arrive at such a late hour?"

"All I want to do is see you."

"Let me in." But he hug her first.

"Are you a newspaper reader?" A newspaper was slammed upon the table by Sanvi. All of them were instructed to get out of the vanity.

"How come I would read it, I don't even buy it?" She chuckles.

"This generation of individuals"

"Don't think that you are the most seasoned member of the generation".

"I notice that, Manya, you misplaced the movie that you were reading a few days prior, even though you still had the date. You were cut off from them now after you split up with Rohit. I am aware that you are unaware that the director's brother is Rohit."

"I had no idea he had so many brothers." Eventually, Manya realized what had transpired.

Sanvi wants to yell, "He was your boyfriend, but you don't know his family, my god."

Manya stood and took a seat on the ground. Weeping and striking his head. "I'm good for the movie, but not for him."

She was in tears. Sanvi does not feel pity.

CHAPTER THIRTEEN

"Have a good day; here's your drink," Manya assumed the appearance of a restaurant employee. She applied makeup and all since she needed to look well for the presentation, but with time, she starts to look terrible. She practiced their operation on the first day. She has received instruction from an Indian restaurant owner. She handled all cooking, cleaning, and cashiering duties. She had a lot more fun with the cashier. There are exchanges and amusing things occur. The kitchen, nevertheless, was the director's favourite. She's not a great chef. She makes mistakes, which gives the audience engaging material. It's a good thing she has staff members supporting her. She usually shows up investigating something in India or going to the jungle, so it may be disastrous. However, she was employed at a restaurant this time. Although the obstacle was overcome, the difficulty has increased. Good and hilarious things are in her nature. Even Americans who are unfamiliar with her were complimenting her friendliness. She could only gaze at the many delicacies that she was being served, despite her desire to eat them. It smells like biryani, and she started to crave chicken.

She spent the entire day shooting, and when it was all over, she was content to flatten on the ground and not eat or do anything except sleep. She became nauseous. She thought it would be so hard to even get to the hotel. She only wants to be transported by magic. Everybody is worn out too. It was even more chaotic than jungle living.

She skipped meals. She fell asleep on the way. As everyone got out of the taxi, she suddenly altered her plans; she wanted to go somewhere else. She used her phone to show the locations because she didn't know how to pronounce them properly. "Yes, this office" it was Danish office. It was lovely. It wasn't for her; it was just a cool place. It made her feel so good to know he was doing well. She was dropped off at the entrance by the taxi. At night, she experienced some nervousness. She didn't walk too far. Her father had given her the boxes for Danish, and she had them. Though she was exhausted from the shooting, she managed to muster the will to see him even though she had already arranged to see him.

She couldn't wait to meet him. Because there was something different about the excitement of really seeing someone. He's been visible to her via video calls. He has terrific looks and different style times. She intended to surprise him by coming up to him so quickly. She waited for him, but it didn't take her long to know that he might take a while. She will eventually have to report herself to security as they won't allow her to enter the properties. She provided her identity card for validation. She called Danish wanted to speak with him at the reception as he had not returned her call. She was aware of his professional commitments. His inclination to work at night persists. The conversation was brief. Perhaps he got aroused too. She considered going to the waiting area to wait. However, he arrived so quickly that she was unable to sit down.

He charged in her direction. And gave her a strong hug. He held her in his arms that she felt her foot in air. Everyone looks to see her unexpected meeting. It was not the same. His smile was equal to Manya's. She chuckled and asked, "Did you jump from your office?" It was a serious question to her. "I was actually heading home." Even though he wasn't hugging her anymore, he was still holding her. She didn't let it go either. "I had a shooting, and I couldn't wait any longer." She was so exhausted that she could take no more. But that was all; he remained astonished and delighted. An extended period of standing wasn't a good idea, as Manya discovered. Danish took hold of her hand. And they leave. "What then should we do?" they find that things change and they are not the same person they were years ago. They were strolling alongside the road. They found it comforting after a long day of labour.

"Have you eaten dinner?" Danish couldn't handle his hunger earlier since he was so excited that he forgot about it. She gave him the gift and nodded in agreement, but it wasn't a good idea to head to the hotel after such a long period had passed. Usually, they converse briefly. She called Danish to decide, who knew more places than she did. After Manya served Indian food all day, they decided to try something different because she was craving something else. They thus demand burritos. As the busiest spot, it was enjoyable for her.

"Hey, Where do you spend the night? It's your shooting day tomorrow." Although she had been avoiding Sanvi for a while, she was still calling. Though she did choose to inform her. She was always so annoying to her. "I promise to return; don't worry."

"Oh, that's great that you have an assistant," he remarked, behaving as though he knew.

She couldn't keep the truth from her; "Cool for me, not for her." Eating the entire burrito quickly, they were both ravenous. Much as she used to, she describes her entire day. Everything she made a mistake with. She also shared recordings of herself being copied with other people. But was unsuccessful. Come to regret performing the show. Danish did nothing but sit and listen to her. She does not stop chatting. He said, erroneously, "Don't you want to go home?" using a Hotel instead of a home. Manya is considering what he is saying for a moment or two. She was ready to dismiss him and say, "Yeah, I should go, but I have never seen your home; I heard you have brought it," but then she noticed how it looked. Danish a great deal; this was not what he expected from her. "Alright."

Since they also consumed alcohol, they took a taxi. A more inquisitive Manya looked about. She enjoyed her surroundings at night. Even though Danish was tired, he continued to watch for her so they might reach their goal. "This is too huge for you," she said to Danish. "Wow" She was startled by the house when the car came to a stop. He remarked, "Not that one sees the right one." She was ashamed; he was not. "It is still. It nevertheless had a large, traditional appearance."

Manya had the impression that her father was with her when he visited her at home and in the city. It was totally opposite. She simply exclaims, "Wow, amazing," whenever she accomplishes anything. "You just don't see a lot." Now, he felt she was exaggerating. The entire motif of the house when she walked in was beige and white; despite the fact that it was night, it was glowingly light. Everything was great and his house smelled great, so he wasn't troubled by anything. To show her, he opened the room. He arranged the kitchen, bedroom, drawing room, and most importantly, the study room, to perfection. It was the focal point of his house, filled to overflowing with belongings. Although a little small, his home was adequate for him.

To obtain ice cream, he went to the kitchen. Manya was scanning the research area. It includes several classics and music CDs. She discovered that in addition to numerous other photos, he carried hers, which he had taken in the hospital. She was giggling as she looked through the pictures, reliving the wonderful moments she had with them. "Ice cream," he remarks after noticing that she had seen everyone's photo. He was proud of the wall and remarked, "I stuck them when I came here; it looked nice." He handed her a cup of ice cream. She continued to gaze at the picture. He was right behind her, in close proximity. There were none between them. Her arm struck his chest as she pivoted. He embraced her. "Are you alright?" He moved a bit nearer. Danish looks mistily into his eyes as their gazes connect. By her waist, he held her. They have closer faces. Their skins can feel each other's breath since they are so near. They both leave at the same moment. She said, "You have a girlfriend," without delay. He was taken aback. "How are you aware of this, but she is my fiancée." He noticed that she was fixated on a single picture of Mandakini, his fiancée. He hadn't told her earlier, which was why he was silent. Holding his head, he apologizes for the setback, saying, "It just hit me." She felt disappointed in Danish as well as in herself. She was astonished to hear, "When you became like a player type." Danish sniff. He was unable to comprehend what he had done.

"I was at a loss for words; you didn't tell me you were getting married, but you should be worried about yourself because you are now making things worse for me and more and more for you, or you should just refresh your mind because you were going to do it and I myself," she said. Danish acknowledges that he did indeed make a major mess. Moving closer to reassuring her, he continued, "Sorry, I can clear it." She remarked, "Stay there; I don't want to become a witch for some women." He immediately refutes.

The bell rung. They both forgot who it would be and what they were talking about. Danish was aware that Mandakini would be the one, but Manya was clueless. She asks him, "Who is it?" before answering the door. "That's her," Slowly nodding, she was already a mess. Act as though nothing occurred.

"Oh, it's a player, she has perfect timing"

"I'm not okay, and I have tell her this before, she really know everything, there is nothing hidden about us"

She gave him a hug as he answered the door. Manya chose to grab an ice cream cone and sat on the couch, behaving as though she was a visitor. When she came in, she was a little taken aback. Greetings, "I'm Manya." She exuded formality, as if she were a teacher. Although they greeted each other, it didn't appear humble. But being quiet is preferable.

"You're here, then." Felt like unwanted.

Manya stammered, "Actually, I came here to shoot here in New York, and then I gave something that my father gave to Danish, so I came here." In real life, being an actress is not helpful for her. She struggle.

"Ah, so what kind of shooting is that?"

"It's just a funny show, a common reality," she says, unable to articulate the meaning.

"How about where you're staying?"

"Hotel, the food and hotel both are fantastic."

She got so many question one by one. She remind her about her English teacher in school, who just hate her a lot. Who she could never impress.

"I'm so sorry, Mandakini, but I was about to kiss Manya." The confession was not a good one. "But you have my undivided love; it was an error that I have corrected." "Danish," both of them yell simultaneously. Mandakini gives up on ice cream. She felt ashamed. Manya wish to flee from this duo. "Do you think this will show how much you respect me, or do you think it will show your honesty?" she yelled. Manya even received a swear. "No, you have my love and respect. I apologize; I'm sorry; I'm just a mess," he broke down in tears. "Indeed, he wasn't correct; it was an error. You had only begun to get to know one other, yet already he was thinking about you, telling me he loved you too much." She made the decision to support her dumb friend, who has since received a new title. "Just shut up, please." Manya faltered. However, she yelled at Manya, which made Danish a little defensive. This infuriated her, and she slung ice cream at her. She yells, "Just get out of his way," and shuts the door. Manya turned back to her sofa and remarked that she had never been tossed ice cream. Danish hurried to grab a face wipe.

She was serious when she said, "It's okay, Danish; you just clean up your mess and stop saying the truth every time."

With her expression remaining fixed, he replied, "I have to be honest with her."

She pulled out her suitcase and stated, "This world will end if people are this honest all the time."

She attempted to offer him strength in case he could figure out a method to handle the unexpected. She rejected his desire to come and see her off. She know how Danish is honest, which is great but his timing was bad.

❧❧❧

"Cut, cut, stop it. Manya, what's up with your angry expression? When you welcome them, you ought to smile." He even taught her how to express herself, yet her expression was monotonous and unchanging. Sanvi could sense something was off. when she returned at night with ice cream all over her hair. She repeatedly inquired, unaware, but she never answered. She simply clarified, "I got a pack for it's just melt," at the end. She didn't elaborate on how her hair may be However, the ice cream failed to calm her down. All day long, she was irate.

"Since it's a reality show, I'm showcasing my true self," she grinned.

"I'm sorry, but I have no interest in following your private life. he gives you a little time to relax and advises, get yourself."

Even though Manya was obviously upset, she maintained her composure. She was clinging to her emotions so as not to jeopardize her closest friend's life. She considered phoning him several times to discuss it, but she finally concluded Mandakini was the one who required an explanation first. His impending marriage was the most unscttling aspect of him. She doesn't remember that; it just occurs to her when things seem dire. She recently broke up. When something happen you begin compiling a list of negative things and ask yourself, "How bad is your life?"

CHAPTER FOURTEEN

She didn't spend much time with Danish throughout her week-long visit in New York. That was the only time she said that out loud. Mandakini was currently okay with things. She was reluctant to trust him at first. Manya thinks it's great that Danish has her in his life, but she also senses that there is a problem he needs to consider about.

Perhaps he will be content. Danish also wanted Manya to understand him, but she was uninterested. She ultimately makes the decision to either quit communicating on a daily basis or simply on their birthday. They felt it would be fantastic every now and then. However, this means that occasionally, they are also ignorant.

Manya chooses for herself that is where the day begins. She wants to go out and have fun, but she never forgets that she is the obstacle in his life. Everything shot perfectly. She must give it her all. When she doesn't make sense and isn't funny, people stop caring about her. She now has a large social media following. Though she wasn't producing many more movies, she was nonetheless entertaining in a number of capacities. She just wants to enjoy herself, at least a little bit; she doesn't want to be too hard on herself. Occasionally, she simply thinks about how much she misses him but is unable to do action. The idea of leaving him for, like, forever made her afraid because they didn't talk much already. She gets a lot of calls from Danish, but she never answers.

It wasn't beneficial to them because, at most, it led to misunderstandings between them. Manya remained silent, acknowledging that she was sort of leaving but missing the times when she could still have fun and could still rely on people. You only need to take care of that on your own.

The movie Manya received has begun, and at last she was cast in a lead role. She was upset that, rather than being selected for the movie because of her talent, she was being famous via the shows. She has constant self-doubt. It's only that after seeing the movie, she lost all memory of it. Merely focusing on the performance. Days after the shoot, she is using old pictures now.

In a few months, half of the filming is finished. She had hoped for a holiday, so it was a relief. Sanvi was busy with a lot of stuff and didn't have time for anything when she was in New York previously. This might really lift their spirits. She also purchased the ticket. So that she can surprise her, run away from her.

"Cut and get change, Manya; we'll start in 15 minutes." Weary from standing all morning, she hops onto the chair. She was in every scene, walking and standing. Even after sitting, she had never felt so calm. She had her head turned to the sky. The sky look beautiful. Sanvi's face materialized out of nowhere; she appeared a little nervous. Manya wait to speak when sitting erect.

"It's imperative that you visit the hospital right away," she stated, biting her lip.

"Why? What took place?" She rose.

"Your father." She ceased to listen and bolted towards the car. Sanvi informed the director over the phone. She reassured her that her father was okay and that he had fainted in the office due to something unsettling. However, he was brought to the hospital right away. Numerous time she considered calling Danish, but she assumed he would also become anxious since he was unable to do so. She made the decision to remain composed and head straight to the hospital instead of making any calls. She senses that everything will work out fine. She simply shut her eyes so that she would be able to act.

Calm yet assertive, she remarked, "What he is experiencing, is he is experiencing pain or a bad stomach."

"I'm not very knowledgeable." His office called me on your phone, saying he fainted and was sent to the hospital right away. She comforted her by extending out her hand and saying, "Don't worry, everything will be fine."

Upon there, they encountered his co-worker, with whom she was unfamiliar. A man approached Manya and said, "Oh Manya, your dad has had a heart attack; he is in the ICU; he will be fine; don't worry." She doesn't want to make herself feel worse, so even though she knows him, she accepts what he says. They were seated. Manya gaze was fixed on the floor. He's got an extremely tense colleague as well. They ought to be quite close, in her opinion. Neither did she ask him to introduce her, nor did she plan to meet anyone. She felt better, and calmer. Good energy would cure others. Everybody fell silent. She holding out for more details on him. Manya doesn't say anything. Her father used to chant Guru Nanak Grant on occasion; she only remembers this Punjabi phrase because of how frequently he used to utter it. She doesn't believe but at that moment she did.

The ICU was suddenly very chaotic, going back and forth as a nurse. There's a loud person outside. Manya lost her composure there. She was aware of what was happening. She exuded positivity throughout. However, she senses bad news. She glances in from the exterior of the space. Her neck swelled and she was broke. Sitting on the floor, she wept as she peered inside the room. Sanvi was unable to stop herself from seeing Manya, just as she was unable to stop herself. She is too weak to comfort. She was astounded by what they had been doing; they had not even considered this possibility. What they could, however, do.

"I am sorry, your father had a silence attack, we couldn't save him"

"Hey, what's up with Danish? Are you able to see him?"

"He has a ten-minute meeting, and then it ends."

"Alright"

There was a loud knocking sound. "What's that?" The chief manager was not amused by the commotion. Danish ignored their disapproval and carried on with his presentation. He was unfazed by her. "I apologize for bothering you all, but Miss Manya called for Danish." She paused and had a dejected expression. That she had finally called him, nevertheless, made Danish glad. Perhaps she wanted to chat to him. That she had altered her mind pleased him. However, he noticed her face, and it confused him.

"Thanks, I see. I'll give her a call right away."

She didn't even know her, but it felt horrible to break the news to him in this way. "Actually, you don't have to; she said to send you this message immediately, just that your uncle has passed away, and that's it," she added. However, she felt that she ought to act swiftly. "I sincerely apologize, Danish."

The Danish appear dismayed. He was unable to comprehend a word she had spoken to him. All he's doing is staring at his laptop screen. And he had everyone's attention. His expression conveys to everyone how broken he was. His eyes began to well up with tears. Perhaps he wish the news was incorrect, but it wasn't.

Manya was silent. In the Pooja, seated. Danish considered seated next to her. He continued to stare at her, countenance unchanging. Her pale skin and watery eyes look depressing to him. She has been this way ever since he arrived: she hasn't spoken to him at all. She was not at all irate. She simply keeps to herself, working on her father's final rites without speaking to anyone.

Danish was always there to aid her. Being the first to arrive, his parents also came. Manya was quiet at the hospital, according to what his Danish mother told him. She sobbed there, but now she is silent and not even crying. Just keep your look neutral—no one was pressuring her. Manya families arrived from both sides of the family, but she had never met anyone and was therefore distant from everyone. She doesn't have any relationships because of this. Sanvi was reliant on her kin. She tried to remove the journalists from her residence when they also visited. It was her phone. Since fewer people were, in a way, speaking strange things that she didn't want Manya to read. But she proved to Danish that unpleasant individuals may exist even when someone is going through their darkest moment. However, they wish to offer opinion about it. She was unable to remove it. On her phone, she simply erased the account.

Manya and Danish's mother assisted in watering the whole region after the pooja. She took it out of the water. The food was not taken by her. He made a lot of requests, but she just sleeted on the living room floor while she sat on her empty stomach. He realized that he had left her alone for a while even though she wasn't sleeping. He knew her family wouldn't even be interested in what she was doing, so he continued to watch her. Since she was aware that Manya wouldn't approve, her mother maintained her distance. Although she tried her hardest to get out of there quickly, her relative lingered at Manya's place. She didn't eat the other day either, but instead she gave meals to people at the Gurudwara. All day, she has been a food donor. She never stopped serving. She worked all day, even though she doesn't have much energy.

When Danish's mother saw her like this, she became tense. She tried to aid her, but soon found that she was powerless to help much. Danish caressed her mother's face and said, "Please don't cry; it will make her more sad." "It feels worry, but Manya didn't smile. I don't want too. When her grandma passed away, she looked like this. She was surrounded by very few people all of her life, and now she is by alone. She doesn't get it, and it's killing me." She sobbed uncontrollably. Maybe they don't have blood relation but she know her from the childhood. She feels her.

Danish realized that Manya would become ill if she went without food, but he was powerless to stop her. He stole the serving bowl and used it as a seat. He presented everything to her and gave her a dish. And give her a little bit more. She was quiet, but she was nonetheless. To ensure Danish seated next to her in order to prevent her from leaving. Her gaze was fixed on the wall. Danish grasp her. She gives him a look. "Manya, please eat." She does eat, but not particularly well. She went out of business. She nibbled on a little bit of everything. Danish didn't protest because he didn't want to push her to improve either, but he was aware that starvation would undoubtedly make her ill.

Even though Manya's previous apartment was small, it was still inhabited, and in some way, Manya's room was used as well. She let herself some space. She was doing the dishwashing in the kitchen. She doesn't have to, but perhaps she was attempting to pass the time. Danish said, "Where are you sleeping?" but all she could do was point to the floor. He suckers. "Okay, take my room. No need. I'm going to be in the living room for a meeting." He answered, "You go to sleep," and took the plates from her. Danish was happy that she didn't object to his actions. She either refuses or accepts silently. No, he didn't make her talk. To force it was just a lousy idea. Allow them time. Being depressed and grieving is normal and not a bad thing.

Danish really had work to do, but even though it was only a fifteen-minute task, he made a lot of effort. Maybe there was a valid reason she felt horrible enough to steal his room, so he told her a falsehood. He was sleeping on the couch without a blanket. He was also having trouble falling asleep. Nevertheless, he remembered a blanket from his room at midnight. When he first entered the room, he was incredibly quiet. "You were unable to sleep," Manya whispered to one another. Danish was quite happy to hear her voice, even though she wasn't relieved. Taking the blanket, he muttered, "Yeah, maybe jetlag." She remarked, rising up, "You sleep here; you would have tried a lot; I am not sleepy; I think I don't want slept." It appeared on her face that she had not yawned. "Manya, I believe you are fatigued as well."

He was ready to go. "It doesn't make sense that none of us is getting any sleep, so we can split it."

They didn't feel very tired. Avoid being too hard on yourself. Manya, remained silent and didn't consume anything. One may weep. It seemed as though a tear fell from her eyes. She doesn't want to say much, but she says, "You're also trying to be strong; your mom is sad; you cried the whole journey, and now." She was simply gazing at the ceiling. Both were sobbing. "You all don't have to act like such strong person."

"I am not," she sobs as the tears escape her eyes. Danish turned to face her; she was longer crying, and she had no intention of stopping. He embraced her. Her face was buried in his chest. Sobbing aloud. Danish lost control after witnessing.

❧❧❧

The Danish get up early. Manya remained in her sleep. They had too much in close. So close to one another that only half of the bed was used. And half was unused. He gazed at her unceasingly. She was soundly asleep. He rubbed her face and as she still stick his chest. He comb her hair from his hand as her hair got messier. Upon up, he noticed the time. Thought of exiting the room, he observed his mother busily engaged in the kitchen.

Some of Manya's relatives were about to leave, so he prepared to assist them. She prefers to meet people at home because she doesn't spend a lot of time in public. She wasn't in the room when he was going to wake her up. She had some people to see. She placed an order for breakfast, which she was serving to each person. "This is yours." She gave Danish one. Now that she was an adult, he was just standing there seeing her perform household chores that she detested. She's taking accountability now and isn't letting it get away from her. She carried on with her work despite having a broken heart. Even though she had no interest in socializing, she nevertheless greeted everyone with wide arms. That is too much to ask, though, since she was unable to cover her face.

Danish didn't like that she used to express herself a lot, but now that she just hides and is so silent, you can't even guess what she is up to. That was the one other thing that changed about her. It wasn't that for him; he misses the way she used to express herself as if she didn't care. He could sense her desires early on, but he now finds it difficult to express them. Even so, he was pleased that she smiled once, albeit slightly, when she does.

Everybody disappears slowly, very slowly. The home was deserted. It's strange to imagine that it was once so chaotic, yet that now it feels abandoned. Manya cleaned up once more with assistance from her maid. It dawned on him to prepare lunch for everyone. He made an attempt to find out what she wanted, but even before that, it is ill-advised to inquire as she is unlikely to respond. He left her to eat and unwind in quiet by herself.

A month has passed. Manya had changed, but at least she had struck up a conversation with everyone. She was grinning and displaying her happiness. Danish and his parents spent a great deal of time with her, but they couldn't stay indefinitely. Danish needs to keep working. It was his mother who had the duty of seeing her frequently. Thus nobody was able to. Manya wasn't making her movies. But she made the decision to start early. She always decides something and then changes her mind.

Danish overlooks the fact that he is engaged in this. He spent many days on call feeling very irate with her. For his job.

"When are you coming?"

"I don't know Mandakini; my parents are also supporting her; she lost her father; nobody is here."

"But Danish, it's been months already. Have you lost sight of your own life while tending to others?"

"How do I make this clear to you? I'm not. I really don't want to discuss it right now, please."

These days, that's how they normally talk. There was nothing she could say to him. Simply put Manya out of his mind, or simply concentrate on himself. She wishes to be less self-centred. She was sure she would figure it out. And chat to him, but she was too busy to consider doing so when he received a call from his office. Thus, he chooses to go. Manya responses weren't negative. To drop him off at the airport, she travelled there herself. In order to avoid being recognized, she covers herself. He is hugged by all. But at that moment, his mother spoke up. "You are doing a fantastic job, Danish, but you still need to make a decision about what you want to accomplish with your life. Since

Manya likes my child as well, I don't want you to play about with her. I simply want us to be happy." Danish had none, so he was unable to respond. It's such a poor moment that everything appears so terrible. No one, however, could alter the time.

❧❧❧

"How do you do this?"

"I often tell you that I am in the middle of the shooting," she said in response to his question for the tenth time.

"Yes, I am aware that I distort words."

"What makes you video call me every day?" When he contacted Manya, she seemed to be feeling better, but now her saddest look is back. He thinks it strange that she shifts her mood so quickly. It was hard for him to divert her attention with anything else. There's not much you can do with just the call. He's been making a lot of effort to keep chatting to her and get her to smile.

Manya began filming a movie, but she stopped in the midst. She was always depressed, therefore it was challenging because the movie was cheerful. But that's not reality; that's her job. She manages it somehow. She simply likes to sleep a lot; she wasn't thinking. She enjoys napping whenever she has the chance. Her stomach won't let her eat as much as she would like to. She was mentally making preparations that she would never be able to finish.

"Come on, Manya, the shoot is ready." Sanvi gave a loud shout. "I'll call you back," she says, implying that she no longer calls herself that, regardless of how much she misses anything; instead, she just keeps things hidden. Every day she has grown more reclusive. She left the scene and headed to where it was. It was like effort for her, trying to smile, breathing deeply, and drawing energy from the environment. She still makes a fantastic cheerleader. "Cut" She ran near the vanity while grinning as she listened to it. Her smile vanished as soon as she noticed her reflection in the mirror after entering. She also misses everyone in her life, but occasionally she misses herself a great deal as well.

She threw up everything and slept so easily because the shooting took a long time and they were staying at a hotel. She slept after a long day of work, and it felt good. But all of a sudden, in the middle of the night, her phone rang. Time to time again, without fail, she did not answer. She was tired, but she could hear the ring now.

"What's now?"

"Why won't you answer my call?"

"Danish, you forgot about the time duration; it's freaking 3 a.m." Danish practically forgot about that, his worry taking over his awareness of day and night. It made him feel both dumb and relieved.

CHAPTER FIFTEEN

Bell rung once more. Looking at each other, Sanvi and Manya decide who will open the door. It is, of course, Sanvi. However, because it was late and they were afraid, nobody got up. The bell rung once more. "How should we proceed?" Manya protected her with a hockey. Can be some crazy fan. "It will all work out," she assures her as she continues. Hide behind the sofa, Manya. Ring came on. She opened up quickly this time. "It's the pizza delivery guy, how much?" she exclaims, quickly grabbing her money. Manya says, "Stupid, we didn't order pizza," as she peeps over the corner. However, the fact that it was Danish there startled her. Making fun of them. They were terrified, though. "Once you arrive can't you tell me," Manya tosses a pillow at him.

He actually got them a pizza. Manya was content to stare rather than eat. She used to eat a great deal. She followed a balanced diet when she began working in the film industry on a professional basis. They both fixed their gazes on each other, and Sanvi was eating pizza. It was the notion, not the hunger that took her out of herself. "What brings you here?" Sanvi, a detective, stated. He never hears from her. They were unable to communicate despite having only met him at the funeral. She senses something fishy about him. But everything had previously been prepared by Danish. "I got a transfer, since I am Indian, they naturally send me to handle the Indian branch for a while." He responded in a way that satisfied. Both gave him a nod of agreement. "What is the total number of days?" was the precise query. "I'll find out about it," he said with a smile. They gave another nod.

"You'll remain here, then."

"No, here at my home."

"Yes, we truly are out of room."

Between, Manya says, "No, you can stay if you want." She appreciated that he was attempting to assist. Although he had no intention of staying, he was pleased that she had even made the offer. Manya walked to her room after giving him a glass of water. Sanvi came running after her.

Sanvi said, "Don't date him," so that he wouldn't hear her.

"Who, exactly, is dating?" Manya simply lay on the bed with her eyes closed.

"You understand what I'm saying."

"I understand, but what if I do? What's the issue?"

"You should date a celebrity; he is not one."

"Don't worry he has a fiancée"

Danish bellowed, "I got a bunch of stuff; just take it; I am leaving." The door opened and Manya saw him standing directly before her. He gave him a large box that looked like a mystery box, and he filled it with various purchases. "I'll let you sleep in the father's room." It astonished him that she would offer. He says, "It's okay, I'm only ten steps away from your apartment."

He was about to leave but he turn back.

"All right, I apologize for listening in on you from outside. Sanvi, I may not be a celebrity, but I sure as hell I am exciting." Sanvi felt ashamed. "I stayed silent because I knew he could hear you."

❧❧❧

"How did you get inside the apartment?" Sanvi arrived early since they were going to the filming location. She was taken aback by her unexpected meeting with Danish. Sanvi figured pretty soon that he was preparing biryani for breakfast which was not an appropriate time. She lunges to see what stage he's at. He laughed and said, "Of course I broke the window and entered it."

She looks at him while standing. "What are you doing here? You come here every day to make food, but you don't have anything or an office." She draws nearer so that she may more easily dispute. Danish merely grinned without saying anything. Rather, he brought her a platter of tantalizingly hot biryani. It arrived on the dish immediately, with the customary quantity of meat and, of course, raita.

He clears his throat and steps in front of her. "Everyone says men's roads to happiness go from stomachs, but no one is talking about women, but I think they want a course of meals," he remarks.

"Are you attempting to flirt with me, oh my god?" She continued to eat quickly.

"I just want you to know that I am here for Manya so she can move on and be normal. A man who treats women well doesn't necessarily want to flirt with you". He finished with a glass of water, saying, "I don't understand that she is doing everything, but she doesn't talk much, stays in her room all day, and doesn't even eat properly, so don't interrupt in between us." Though they are no longer as close as they once were, Sanvi is aware of his worries for her. She doesn't think anything has gone wrong because of this. After his arrival, they didn't talk at all.

"All right, I get it. But could you also try to stop interrupting during the workday?"

Suddenly, Manya left the room. It gets difficult for them both, and she becomes suspicious. She entered the kitchen immediately and saw that, true to her statement from yesterday, he had prepared biryani. However, she rejected it. Intercom ranged. "You made me anxious when the bell rang." Sanvi moves to let herself in. And there's old man in a lawyer suits in his 50s waiting at the door. His first request is for Manya. "What went wrong," she whispered, snatching his shirt and ducking behind him. To go in front of her, he grabbed her wrist. Danish decided to strike up a discussion. He approached the door. The attorney uttered his name aloud. It startled Danish that he recognized his name; perhaps they were acquainted. But he was unable to identify it. He apologized, saying, "I didn't recognize you," to ensure they would identify him when he entered. Manya takes a backward glance.

"It's actually my fault; perhaps you overlooked me. I'm Bali, the personal attorney of Manya's father, and I'm also a friend. I'm here to discuss everything about real estate." All are aware of the circumstances. They didn't anticipate having a lawyer show up at their door in the morning. They welcomed him in. They sat at the dining table, which seemed strange. For a stranger but Danish gave him a small portion and also served Manya after he pleaded for biryani. He started removing some papers from a bag he had. In her father's room, she also took some paper.

"You have to realize that everything belongs to your father, in my opinion. Although I know the timing wasn't ideal, I considered giving you this paper sooner. Well, these are the ones that will be transferred to you, but the most of the paper you may have already."

It's incomprehensible that despite listening to everything, she wasn't interested in her. She did, however, nod in agreement with everything, including his request for a personal meeting. Mostly replies from Sanvi and Danish to him

"Yes, your bungalow in Punjab is not in your"

"Oh, yeah, mom, that makes sense. She always love that house"

"No, it's actually for Danish"

Everyone is staring at him. He began to panic. "How am I to blame?" He remarked, "I think you should check again," and took the papers to be checked. Sanvi sent him a menacing look. "I know you may not be aware of this, but he claimed that when you were younger, you shattered his pricey clock, but you didn't say I'm sorry; instead, you responded, I'll get this home, so he wants to give you something. You were like his child, I know he desired for you," he remarked, proving to him that it was indeed the case. He was taken aback and wavered, reluctant to take the risk. He handed her the paper and added, "Okay, I never said this; thank you, but I give it to her." "No, it's for you, and you said that," she did remark. Manya's decision to give up her home because her father wanted to offer someone else a "Wow, I think he came because of this" startled Sanvi. He deny right away.

"I won't interfere, but you need to talk to each other and let me know," he said as he turned to go. Manya was eating, at least, even though she wasn't in anything. Danish gathered the papers and placed them in her chamber without making any noise. Suddenly, though, Manya called him. "I'd like to speak with you." She was just eating, though, and not conversing with him. He thus permitted her to watch her eating show similar to her reality shows. She was too ashamed to even speak, head down, "Let's just sell the house." What she just said startled Danish. Despite his anger, he refrained from yelling. He inhaled deeply. Trying not to lose his cool, he asks, "Now what are you up to, Manya." "Nobody is here; you can see who is going to live there; no one here even peeks in there," she said, glancing at him. "You take the money, no problem, but don't have it; just sell it," she said.

"I don't like to hold on to stuff, you know." Her head remains lowered.

"So, too, sell this." he said, "Oh, that's a really good idea," sounding irate.

Danish was at a loss as to how to approach her. They sometimes argue when she speaks, even though she doesn't say much. He gave his head a scratch. He declared, "I won't sell the house; I don't want money." This time, he showed no emotion at all. He was heading inside the room. She stopped him and said, "Okay, fine, don't be a kid; that's not a big deal." "That's great, but I need to transfer to you; please set aside a few days for that." This time, he disregarded her advice.

❧❧❧

"Why must I accompany you here?" Sanvi fumbles with his camera and bag.

"Why are you filming this? Do you think there's anything exciting here?" Manya yell at Sanvi. Life is terrible. Manya wasn't in the finest frame of mind to talk; the little discomfort can turn into a major drama.

"Don't judge others by looking around; instead, just have fun." Bags were taken by Danish.

"Oh, that sort of fixes everything."

"I told you repeatedly not to argue with her"

Danish laughs at Manya despite the heat, the environment, and their own passionate disagreement. Despite her angry expression, he found her appearance amusing. She covers her face and head with a black sunglasses. She exudes cool Indian rural style. "So what?" The giggle annoyed her. "Nothing, just enter the room." The bungalow's main door was closed, but the house's entrance gate was open. Their caretaker was supposed to arrive, so they placed their bags there, but they could enter inside. After waiting a long while, they made the decision to explore. The elderly woman had lived in the residence. The house was gone, sadly. Moving to the city, they did. They survey the area and conclude that, based on what they can tell, he resides somewhere.

"DON'T GO IN, NO ENTRY, okay get into this" Manya enter the property fast. Ignoring the board. Sanvi and Danish simply yelled "Hey" at her, but she ignored them. "The owner will yell there, so stay away," said a man approaching from behind. At last, they received the caretaker. "Don't go there; there are a lot of animals there." Getting the directions didn't pique her attention.

Manya cautioned Danish, saying, "I said for the hotel that it was your idea to live here."

"Well, alright, I get it."

"I apologize; it took a long time. After sending my daughter to school and delivering milk, I had to go to the government office today." He said, "I am getting a free machine for my farm."

"You seem to have a well-organized life, Mahesh ji; I'm envious." Sanvi was enjoying the rustic atmosphere now. It was a different kind of holiday for her; she never had a village and never travelled to any.

"There's a ton of work. Numerous stop in between. She abruptly introduced Danish by saying, "He is the owner of this house." He shocked. Denied. He was blind by her, he approached for the greeting. "No, I'm not; let's just get comfortable before I get some snacks for the two of us."

❧❧❧

Danish assumed the task of preparing the meal. The Danish wanted to make batti chokha, the dish that Manya's grandmother used to cook with cow dung, but Manya didn't want to help and insisted on eating dinner somewhere in Dhaba. Sanvi is helpful; despite her ignorance, she lends a hand to him. When she found out about the cow dung made, she became appalled because she assumed it was just dirty mud. She declined to consume it. Finally, he began working on it himself. He added potatoes and tomatoes, smeared the brinjal with oil, sliced it open, and added some garlic. Sanvi recorded everything on camera. She had captured every moment of the journey on camera. Attempting to capture the greatest possible photos.

"This needs to be uploaded." Sanvi yelled, "Manya, come join," but she disregarded him. Danish at least requested assistance, but he received none. He was kneading dough and smearing with water. It was Manya who washed the floor and arrived at last. "All right, this is the best; let's introduce ourselves, and I'll start the video," said Sanvi. Both decline right away. Cameras are routine for Danish. The main reason he was afraid of is that they make fun of him in videos. The exception to his dislike of attention is Manya. She kept asking, "Please," nonstop.

"How about just posting a video of yourself cooking?" Danish has second thoughts.

"You don't like cameras? This is a sudden change," Manya said in shock.

"All right, let's begin by introducing ourselves," Sanvi enters the scene.

Greetings, "This is Sanvi, the manager."

"I'm Danish, the neighbour."

"Hello, I'm Mahesh..," she said, pointing to the knife.

"No, that's not how you say it; go back and start."

Manya shoved Danish aside to speak. Thus, he presents the entire situation. Despite his lack of knowledge, he performed well. "It seems like you are overcooking the potatoes. Even though she could have saved those potatoes, she chose to just observe since it was not her job. Danish leaps to its defence. By luck, a few were unharmed. Sanvi stressed that the video should be engaging, but there was quiet. Manya learns how to make batti from the Danish. Forming the ball and stuffing the dough. Part of the challenge was that they were cooking it the old-fashioned way. She tossed the batti and remarked, "I want to sleep with an empty stomach; if I knew that it would take years to make, I would reject it right away." staring at Sanvi, who didn't really assist them because after that she was so focused on shooting.

"I just finished. They all seem cooked, so I'll help you out now." After applying a small amount of ghee, they were finished. Sanvi prepared the scene for the audience by starting the plating and setting the camera for the time lapse. They offer the evaluations. Manya said to Sanvi, "I think you should just say it's good because it barely helped us."

"I agree with you, boss."

CHAPTER SIXTEEN

Sanvi posts the video online. Their entire voyage was captured on camera, and it was entertaining to watch because they weren't acting and were just sharing their childhood friendship—something no one had ever seen. It was the first time Manya had ever had a close relationship with her. Viewers become curious about it. However, Sanvi made a small error that was too obvious on numerous occasions when Danish was staring at Manya, who simply smiled. In the video, that was rather evident.

"Manya, I have a question for you. Everyone is excited about the movie and anticipates impatiently for it because of the response to the trailer."

"Definite I am extremely delighted with respond to, I simply want to stay up with their expectation." Manya don't want to respond to further questions, but other people were speaking as well. Since director was there also who wrote the screenplay also, the film's director provides a brief character explanation. Manya playing the lead role. She didn't show, but she was ecstatic nonetheless. It will be the first time she appears alone on the poster. She understood it all because of how popular she was and how much attention she was receiving. In some way, her career was aided by reality shows. Her only complaint was that she wasn't having fun. That's what was lacking there; she made a lot of effort to focus on what was being presented and to get in the right frame of mind.

"Manya, I saw your video that you uploaded. It's the top trending video given how clever and funny it is, but people want to know about your friend Danish." Once more, Manya is questioned given that she didn't anticipate that. She understood the context, but the video baffled her. She immediately has the thought that Sanvi might be the one who posted anything viral on social media.

She paused. "I understand what people are thinking, but that's what matters—he's my childhood friend, and we have memories together that I had no idea my manager would share." Ended with the smile. She hope it satisfies everyone's need. She objects to the topic shifting from the movie to her personal life. She sidesteps these inquiries and takes the easy one. She didn't become upset since she didn't want to become depressed. She needs to look stunning for the media. And she's done a fantastic job thus far. In some ways, working on numerous projects benefited her. Sanvi, however, is going to have a very bad time because Manya refused to upload the video, but she did. She now has to deal with the fallout.

❧❧❧

Danish try to speak up, "I just want my pictures down, I don't like it." He enjoyed a sandwich made by Manya and Sanvi. However, Danish was depressed about his first experience with paparazzi. He was only buying veggies when they appeared out of nowhere and acknowledged him. He tried to hide his identity from himself, but it didn't succeed. Manya's sole response was, "First of all, next time, wear a mask, please." Danish found it offensive. All he wants to do is remove the picture. Sanvi questioned, "But why don't you deny when they ask you are her brother." Spitting facts, "I think because I am not."

"No, they were merely playing you." They both said sink.

Danish reminds him of the moment when he was being repeatedly and deliberately questioned, perplexing him. He can now understand that they are deceiving him. They expected him to respond. His worry changes as he says, "They made me so conscious that I forgot to buy potato." Both of them done with him. Sanvi know he is only one who cooks, so she is aware of their suffering.

"All right, I'll place the food order," Manya said.

"Great idea, but I have to go to the office tomorrow and I'm not in the mood." Sanvi felt let down.

"You have a temporary job that has turned into a daily routine," Manya suspects. Forget about his work; since moving to India, he has hardly discussed keeping it a secret. Not even Manya inquire about him. He was a skilled concealer. Manya was preoccupied with her own problems and forgot about his possessions. Undoubtedly, someone will eventually become aware of his actions. And he waits for that to happen before facing it. He wasn't thought about an explanation. Like Manya, he was confused at all times. Other than he cannot do much like he cannot change his work so quickly like where he wanted. But still he was granted what he asked for even. Even though they don't operate that way, they still give him a transfer. He was going regular from the beginning of his days after moving from U.S.

"I joined because I got this job." Not a very good justification. How might someone be persuaded of this? He worked at the main headquarters of the company in the United States, so why would someone move him to a branch office? He was working on his primary task. Neither of them seemed satisfied with his response.

"That's strange, but why did you come here? do you remember you were getting married to a woman named Mandakini," she said, recalling everything in case he forgot. He truly forgot about the Mandakini, therefore it was a nice idea to remind him.

Following their breakup. When Danish saw her, he apologized for everything. He believed she deserved a heartfelt apology. He was aware that even if he were to leave her, the pain and memories would remain. When she remembers their time together, it will enrage her. He wanted an honest, unfiltered conversation with her. And give voice to her opinions. In order to prevent her from feeling empty, she needs to say certain things. Despite his extreme meanness against her, he doesn't want to part ways badly.

It was still unable to remove the Mandakini. She had done a great deal of planning for their future, but all of it was lost due to Danish uncertainty. Nevertheless, it's preferable to inform her of his predicament rather than playing with her emotions.

He reasoned that he should leave her in that state so she could reflect and realize that the partnership depends on both of their interests.

He was gradually saying, "If I say that I am not marrying and my job got transferred here," but it was making her confused and upset. His contradictory statement confused her. She was furious and said, "Danish, what are you talking about? I'm not getting anything."

He realized that Sanvi was also present, but he wanted some time alone from the group decision. "You were here alone, so I thought I should come back and yeah again, I got confused that obviously Mandakini didn't like it. Actually we had to prepare for marriage, but that time I was in India that made her pissed which was right because I think I am stupid guy in this I shouldn't have brought life to this, I feel like stupid everyday couldn't even think what should I do about just like you I am also going with the flow," he said.

Sanvi realized she should leave and said, "I think I should go." However, Manya felt terrible because she had never spoken to him about his life. She wished for him to live a perfect life. However, a girl once again left him because of her. She has the shame of it, not even repair it now. Not a good comment that She made: "Make things clear with her; you don't have to babysit here and leave everything." Her remark about how he felt about babysitting didn't set well with him.

"Maybe you don't need me, but I couldn't handle it. I made this decision for myself. Ever since the childhood, you've driven me insane and I can't bear to live with you or without you," he sniffed.

"I apologise; I'm really crazy."

"Can we just continue to be happy and normal like we were when we were teenager"

Her realization that their arguments were making her sad. She knows somewhere that things have changed, but she refuses to acknowledge it. She would like to know if the changes are positive or negative, or if they re-learn. We may believe that we have mastered something because we are constantly learning new things on different stages, so we should arm ourselves with the best knowledge, but then a new problem arises, and we have to learn new things again and again. Thus, once we have mastered. Perhaps when we truly understand happiness?

Maybe that never happen.

They each gave each other a few days apart. They required some time away from shouting to reflect. Whereas Manya was upset since she thought she was hurting Danish's life, Danish regretted his decision. She was aware of how crucial it was for him to travel to the United States, and despite being away from his family, he managed to work there for many years without going giving up. He accomplished so much that he was able to unwind and recuperate, yet he continued. Although she doesn't want him to jeopardize his profession, she can't help but be thrilled that he was there all the time because he came. To prevent her from feeling alone. She is aware of his appreciation for this.

Although they saw each other every day, they remained silent. However, Danish has messaged her numerous times to transfer the property since he is genuinely afraid of it now that he owns it. She disregards his advice. He was taken aback by how much she trusted him to not misuse it. The primary object he want to relinquish control of. Even though her father gave it to him, he doesn't believe he deserves it. It felt to him like a crime. She has been ignoring it ever since they found out about it.

Apart from the vlog, the trip was a complete waste. They were not persuaded to sell it. Danish was not on board with it. They didn't come to any conclusion then being as it is. Danish was aware that she was simply acting too emotionally and wasn't paying attention. He was confident after sometime she will regretted it and blame him because he didn't stop her. He denied entry to the buyer. He politely declined the offers. He reasoned that he should remain silent until she acknowledged her own actions. He will then transfer the residence. He wants to maintain their relationship as it was when they were younger till then.

"I assume your father gave the house to Danish to tell that you should get marriage to him," Sanvi speculating why his father change the will. Manya and Danish felt uneasy about her conjecture. After a long time, they both got together for supper because of Sanvi. She just got into relationship for which she phoned the folks who shouldn't be called at last on this globe for the relationship advices. Their relationship is painful for both of them. All they can do is provide the rationale for ending the relationship.

For Sanvi's benefit, they both kept their mouths shut so she could pursue her happiness. But she intended to wreck her life herself. Not worthy of a call in a fancy restaurant.

"I'm not marrying this guy for a house," asserts Manya. Danish found it really annoying to hear inebriated women converse. In reality, they are only drawing attention to his flaws. He don't have energy to quarrel with them rather than enjoy his drink.

She went on, "Sanvi, you should make other friends because we're going to live alone for the rest of our lives and you'll end up like me." Danish concurs with his entirely. He was full and wanted to go home. He was nearing his breaking point with their pointless banter. Instead, he pulled his phone out of his pocket and took a picture of Manya which she finally poses in.

"I think" Danish intervene in between them. He believed that if he said something in between, they would end up making the wrong choice. "I believe there is no such thing as a perfect relationship; there will always be things that make you doubt it, but all you can do is work together to identify the issue and find a solution. You people always portray couples in the best possible light, but in reality, there is no such thing as a perfect couple; we always hurt and argue with one another, but the most important thing is that in the end, you should come together and hustle hand in hand."

The two girls, who had been staring at him, burst out laughing. Both were drunk badly. Manya smirked and remarked, "You are the one who left from the middle of marriage."

He got up to pay and to head home early. "That's what I did, I was the problem and knew it and solved it, at least I am aware about my problem," he said. He don't want to argue. He want his comfort zone even though he wasn't upset. He was worried about paparazzi would be there to capture him. However, the rain came to their rescue. Because the restaurant was so crowded, they were oblivious to the wind's unusual direction. Staying longer felt risky for the media. Danish's clothes were destroyed and he had to struggle to get inside the vehicle.

He couldn't discover himself anymore because he was already too depressed about life. However, he took the two women safely. They were both straying from the subject whenever they felt like it. Danish steer clear of them because to the loud music, which becomes louder every time they annoy him. Manya was quietly contemplating that she only knew about it when she dropped by Sanvi.

She looked at her phone to make a call and remarked, "I think you still like me, but the difference is you don't like me like before you used to do". His cell phone rang. He took a call. "You are speculating, I didn't say anything," he responded, hanging up. She kept calling, but he kept hanging up. "Why is he not answering?" as if she were unaware of his being beside her. Danish grab her both hands and tells her to quit acting strangely. He didn't let her come out on her own when they got home. To ensure that she stays still, he extended his own hand. However, she locks herself in the car instead. She proceeds to lock it, and he proceeds to unlock it. They move in time, but as she loses it, he opens the door right away. She makes an attempt to flee. But she was drowsy when he grabbed her from behind. He was eager to get home. He still struggles for everything. He dug through her entire luggage to find the key. He had everything he didn't need, but he was missing the key. Manya pounded her shoes to lock it, and in that instant, it opened. Although he never witnessed her do it, he is unable to inquire at this time.

She came in by herself; she didn't require his assistance, so he left her alone. He was still perplexed by the moist floor. Water was present everywhere. Though how could it be rainwater in the apartment, he wondered. Manya walked into the splashing all over the place, not caring. Danish was trying to figure out where it originated, but it was much more. Manya lets out a loud "Ahh." He couldn't believe that her strange behaviour was the only reason it wasn't serious. However, he continued to rush in her direction. They noticed that the water was up to their ankles in her chamber. The drainage system was stopped, but it was coming from the balcony since it was so large.

Manya sits on the floor, devastated that her entire room has been destroyed. However, Danish rushed to open the lid, not understanding why it was so near and close. Water moves very slowly. He observed Manya as her shoes were completely destroyed by the water. He tried to stop her, saying, "I will give you this same I will find". She turned to face him angrily and said, "It was limited edition." It felt right, so he remained silent. He then removed items from the floor that appeared to be damaged or were about to be damaged.

Manya's water cure for hangovers also tries to improve things fast. She had no right to complain as she was the only cause of this negligence. Since the shoes were on the ground and heavily soaked, she decided to save them first. Her phone falls into the water, her pocket tingles, and she tiptoes over. She swiftly grabs the floor and tosses her shoes back onto the bed. She yelled once more.

"Not again," he said as he visited her once more. Fortunately, it was functional. "Please take your time," Danish warned her, making sure she didn't make any mistakes while it was operating. All of a sudden, it stop working. Once more, he was setting things aside. He looked over and saw her wailing for her phone. She was fighting to survive, but it was impossible. She hurried to put her phone in the rice and checked, but it was still not working. Even after the room's water had evaporated, everything remained damp. She really has fewer amenities in her extremely ancient flat than in other high-tech apartments. Despite this, she is unwilling to alter it due to her father's recollections.

She gave him her phone and said, "You are an engineer; can you fix this?" Danish asked whether she was still intoxicated. Despite not being an electrical engineer, he chose to be courteous to her. She simply wants it fixed, though. "Engineer, engineer, same little thing still."

He is too shocked to argue more. He made an attempt to check at least once but was unsuccessful. Thus handed her phone. "This one is yours, take mine ," but she declined since she wanted her. "I want mine with everything in it," she says as she heads to her room to set other items aside. She constantly muttered to herself that because of her negligence, this could have happened. Danish relief that she brought it up at all.

She pulled a fast one, saying, "My phone all its memory." He wanted to help her, but he wasn't able to and wouldn't even guarantee it. She desires full grantee status.

He tries to change the subject by saying, "I will try tomorrow, don't worry, look your hand cleaned in the water and you are sober now" he is one who can make weird comments and laugh on it. "Indeed!" She physically held her hand to his face so he could read the fake stupid. "Everyone says these lines show your future and how are we, I think here it written Idiot," she said.

"I don't think your hands are beautiful see this place is clean."

"Yes, I like my future, tidy."

She sobs aloud at his acceptance of her. He was okay, had a lot in the middle of the night. By the time she drank her last drop. Once she was cleaned, she slept soundly.

He was desperate to go to sleep, but his thoughts prevented him from doing so since he felt empty. Even though he knows she is having difficulties, she will constantly tell him she is okay, but she really misses her father and spends a lot of time at this house, imagining him in everything. However, neither of them expressed their emotions. He spends much of his time on the sofa, in his room, and in the kitchen. He used to read the newspaper, watch TV, and reprimand Manya there because he loved it. But everything vanished the day he went from there.

He occupied the sofa by sitting there. However, he was unaware when he fell asleep there.

"What's wrong with your face?" Manya asked, glancing at his cheeks, which were covered with all the embroidery off her sofa. He sighed as he peered in the mirror. Manya chuckles because the pattern was flawless. Quickly clicked a picture. She has already exposed her entire wardrobe to the sun. She prepared a delicious breakfast as well. They were attempting to figure out how to enjoy themselves, which is why they were being silent.

"I enjoy the quietness"

He didn't seem dejected when he said, "Back then we beg you to be silent but I really miss your talkative, hyper you," instead they both acknowledged that times had changed. And that's just the way it is; sometimes you have to go on and sometimes you can return to things when necessary. At last, Manya was eating enough. She continued to lose weight despite being already quite slim, courtesy to her movie.

Danish handed her his phone because he already owned another one. Though she was impatient and needed her phone immediately in the morning, he handed his to her instead of the one she was considering buying. She didn't took the phone in the night. She swiftly opens her social media account and looks through his, but she doesn't find anything interesting enough to slide in.

This year was both the best and the worst for her since she received her first break in the movie business, but she also lost her father, for which she will never be compensated. Though her film was receiving a lot of attention, she was unable to appreciate it. She was receiving film on the other hand, but this time she received far higher value. Additionally, reality show producers hope to work with her again on a future season. She was becoming confused about her options. She was planning to do both, of course. Danish assist her with the script on the free day. He didn't demonstrate his understanding of these concepts, though. He was still attempting to comprehend her line of work since he wanted to make a difference in her life. However, he enjoys watching the show that brought Manya great joy. They both get the day off. So, in order to occupy their time, they decided to go food shopping.

Manya swiftly loads the cart with the prepared meals that suit her best. Danish was rearranging items from the rear, which he considered to be waste. She spent so much time work that she hardly went outside. She never gave these little things any thought, and here now she found it enjoyable.

In a cutesy way, he continued, "You are so easy to kidnap." he lean forward. She was lost in the grocery shop. Because she was having trouble deciding which flavour of cream biscuits to eat. So she was lost in the market.

She was explicit, saying, "Give your all money if that happens."

"Now what do you want to have for dinner?" he asked, still a little hungry but a little done himself.

She genuinely said, "After 25 years of eating, I'm tired and don't know what to eat, I don't crave anything."

"This makes no sense"

"Well, so you'd like to travel somewhere"

"No, I'm not feeling it"

"You requested coffee"

"I decided against it; it keeps me up at night"

Danish had enough of asking and receiving. She had no idea what it was she wanted to do. Danish then pointed to a mango ice cream, to which Manya promptly consented. As they stroll beside the ocean, she talks to him about the previous time they shared ice cream, which she regrettably ended up eating. For this reason, she tangled her hair. A call comes in for Manya. She opened her own photo by mistake. She noticed that Danish had created an entire album with all of her childhood photos in it. Danish becomes aware of this and tries to grab her hand. She didn't give up though. Began to look at the entire image. It was so many that she was unable to see them all. Danish tried to reunite with some of his childhood memory, but he gave up and sat with her to look at their pictures instead. It brought back every memory and brought her father back to mind.

She didn't like one of them, so she said, "Why you have ugliest picture of mine?"

"Those are unprocessed images."

"Wow, that's how you hope to win my approval"

"It has to be genuine," he laughed.

Manya has been learning to cook since the year. She moved very slowly, making sure every step was correct. Danish had to leave the station for work after many days. Thus, it was quite odd to be by herself for a day. She is typically surrounded by Danish who constantly advise her on what to do and don't do. She is grateful for the extended work he put forth. She still feels strange about him. They had another talk before he left for the airport about returning to the United States, but he didn't listen and insisted on making his own decisions. He realizes when he's with her that it's only about her and that he wants to stay. He has been working so hard to succeed that he hasn't had time to enjoy himself, but now he is too terrified to do so. He was having fun in Manya's acting life. Because she is familiar with the entire industry, he always listens to her stories about the other actor. She considered getting back together with Shresth, Kartik, Yash, and Niti, but none of them could make plans to do so. Even though he still doesn't like them, he thought seeing her old acquaintances would be refreshing.

A baby's cry reached Manya's door. She opens the door before Niti even knocks. Their friendship wasn't very strong before, but these days they support one another. She went directly to the sofa since she wanted to sit and was tired of holding her child. Her daughter embraced Niti in her arms. Manya tried to say "Hey" to grab her attention, but all she got was side looks. She wondered if she would forget her once more. Niti doesn't usually visit, but she wanted to provide her some assistance.

Manya's film, for which she had been waiting a long time but was unable to celebrate, went really well. "How been these days, you got an award I thought to congratulate you," she said. The question was challenging for Manya—in fact, it's challenging for everyone. She continues, saying "FINE!!!"

Niti surveyed her apartment. Everything was different and everything was clean. Her daughter and she check the entire room. "How come?"

Manya with a glass of water behind her. "Do you employ a maid?" she said, taking the glass and giving her daughter a sip.

The doorbell went up.

"This is the maid."

Danish arrived rather early. He came to get the key, which is why he stayed at the doorway; he wanted to get to his apartment as soon as possible. After traveling, he felt exhausted. Niti test the preview. It shocked her to see Danish again after all those years. She hadn't met him well when she'd seen him previously. They greet one another awkwardly. Taking the key, he walked off. Niti gets to work swiftly preparing things in her mind.

"What's he up to here?" She thought quickly to provide the correct response or craft a compelling narrative.

"It's because of me that he returned". She went with honesty. Niti gave a nod.

"I've heard that the will includes Danish."

"You knew he was here, I see". She gave another nod.

"I wanted to make sure but actually Sanvi, who told me that your father had given him your ancestor's house, was telling the truth." It surprises Manya that she is so detail oriented. Sanvi's involvement in all of this was expected. She sighed, ignoring her question. She expected her to delve deeply. And she'll make it easy to find out. She was attempting to get her daughter to sleep in the meanwhile. Since Manya had nothing from the morning, they quickly ordered shawarma for them. Although Shawarma didn't satisfy her hunger, it was nevertheless a welcome reprieve compared to before. "You disregard my inquiry, it's really terrible," she said, refusing to let her go. "I don't think he will sell the property because he has this much dignity," she said without a second thought. Niti was taken aback by her faith in him. She approached her and said, "You think he's here for your property or for you." Manya retreated a bit. Extend her brows.

"You ought to question him."

"Wow, I don't know how long I've been seeing him around you. You dated everyone but not him. I don't know what's wrong with him; after all, he's been with you for so long that he could go back and have a great life in the States, but he's here with you, taking care of everyday things and even pursuing a career."

"I am a bad person," Manya said, not sure if it was a true statement or just a slip of the tongue.

Niti continued to attempt to be modest with her, saying, "No you not you are just stupid." "I don't do it specifically, but I never felt like that in the past. It feels like there might be something, but I'm afraid because I now see how people get scared of something that seems so simple."

The doorbell abruptly interrupted her. She realized who will be since Danish ring a bell with different style. She recognized him, but what was strange was that he use to entered the house without much knocking. She acknowledges that he might have wanted to let them know he was at the door. He brought his food from takeout with him. Something to let them know about. "I also purchased some strawberries." He had the energy to turn the conversation to food. To serve the food, he headed to the kitchen. Manya had the idea to assist in cleaning the strawberries. She rose in the water-filled bowl and drained it afterwards. She swiftly removed the leaf and nibbled onto it. "Oh, it tastes sour." She gave a strange look. Danish tasted it too, and found it to be sour. "I apologize; you're being bothered by everyone a lot. Please don't give in to the pressure, or I won't sell your property." His remarks made the strawberries taste less sour to her. That he was concerned about her felt good. She simply grinned broadly. Considering what he learned from their chat. He must have her things also. Manya was fed up with so audible flat.

"You must be hungry, let's eat."

CHAPTER SEVENTEEN

"I had no intention of doing this."

"Welcome to the world of Manya. I travel in this manner every year. I ought to have voiced my displeasure more, but I refrained from doing so." Sanvi has accommodated herself remarkably well to Manya, to the point where she has become similar to her. Since Danish's birthday is still coming up, he decided to throw a party in honour of it.

Even though he was yearning for a trip, he was unable to go on his own. He does not possess the ability to produce an atmosphere that is both enjoyable and energizing. When he travels with his parents, it is similar to a school trip in that he is required to get up early, finish all of his assignments on time, travel to all of his places within the allocated time, arrive at the hotel on time, and then go to sleep. He decided against going on vacations with his family as a result of all of these issues. He had the idea to stay at home and find something to do with Manya, but he wanted it to be a private affair rather than one that included everyone else.

Because of this, he chooses to disregard everyone's inquiries on his birthday. He claims that it was a typical day in the neighbourhood. On the other hand, he had a deep-seated desire that it not be like any other day. As a straightforward yet warm birthday celebration, he considered the idea of preparing meals and going to the movies with her. He did not picture her as his closest companion; rather, he envisioned her as his partner, which is a scenario that is highly improbable to take place.

However, he destroyed the illusion that he had created in his head when he realized that there had been no interaction between them as of yet. Nevertheless, there were particular aspects of their relationship that were so optimistic that they experienced a sense of normalcy, just as they had in the past. At this point, Manya is paying attention to him, and they are no longer irritated with one another. Even though they were going through challenging times, they both maintained a positive attitude in spite of their difficulties. Due to the fact that things were not going according to plan, they made the decision to go their separate ways. The act of merely pondering on oneself without making any attempt to seek approval from others.

Manya intended to carry out the shooting in Dehradun. There will be a week during which she is not at home. In addition, she desired to celebrate his birthday in that location. Nevertheless, he had a very minor fear regarding the manner in which he would interact with the public. It is highly likely that there will be a significant number of individuals present. Also, he is unable to disregard everyone. On the other hand, after giving it a great deal of thought and contemplation, he ultimately decided to go along with them. She had a good relationship with Sanvi, and Sanvi was a settled individual. Sometimes, Manya finds it unsettling to ask herself, "Am I not making the necessary efforts?" This question causes her to feel uneasy.

He pushes her to respond, "Actually, I am her oldest friend, so I think I better know her than you."

She reminded him that she had learned to be a savage from his closest buddy by patting him on the shoulder and saying, "Yeah, we know you are the oldest here, and we really respect you, Uncle"

They were about to board. Manya was not afraid because there were so many crew members that no one suspected her of anything. She was freely talking to Danish. She attempted to persuade him to purchase the liquor, but he declined. Even though Danish agreed to come along, he was with everyone. He is always at the back or in a corner somewhere. Manya also doesn't push him forward; he was already doing things from a comfort level, and she doesn't want to make things hard.

"I don't see why you are so worried about being discovered." The question was posed by him as he moved a bit further away from the group, which led her to become concerned. "Seriously,

I am not dating," she responded with self-assurance. "We are not dating," he inquired. So he took her hand in his. This time, she was not. "Keep your hand away from me." She attempted to withdraw, but she didn't really put in a lot of effort or effort at all. "Take it easy."

A few meals were prepared for both of them him and Manya. However, he was unaware of how to pick up a donut, despite the fact that he want one. Nevertheless, Manya, who was familiar with the fundamentals, picked it up very fast. While he continued to hold her hand, he dragged her finger to the menu with the intention of making a decision for himself. Because the airplane is prone to being late, she arrived in a hurry and said, "He'll have the same."

Despite this, he was relieved that he was able to secure the seat next to her. He had made the decision to not leave things up to fate, and now he was taking charge of his own life. He was uncertain as to whether or not this was God's plan or his own. "I can't eat that much; why do you buy so much?" he asked.

The sweetness caused his eyes to brighten and widen, and Manya could just gaze at him. "You can watch me," he added as he took a piece out of the donut.

It took quite some time for them to board the ship, and she became bored. Although she travels quite a bit, there are times when the journey can be exhausting. Danish, as is his custom, maintains his composure and waits patiently for the process to be completed. He does not frequently express his displeasure, but Manya has frequently thrown tantrums. It was not even business-class, and she was going through the worst. "Just don't shout again; everything will be fine," he says repeatedly, which assists her in maintaining her composure. Less than a minute passed before she was sound asleep. When he finished typing on his laptop, she leaned on his shoulder and leaned back. He was able to type more slowly as a result of her presence. When he slipped into her trap, however, he promptly fell asleep as well.

They had both separated themselves from the rest of the crew. It seemed as if they were reliving the good old days. After a period of time, they arrive to a state of tranquillity and stability.

It was upsetting to learn that they would be shooting as soon as they landed down, despite the fact that the flight had been so extensive. Danish had already made up his mind that he wouldn't bother them. He devised a strategy to investigate those regions. He is already aware of the fact that shooting does not provide him with any entertainment. Rather of trying to impose one's preferences on other people, Manya reminded him that it is significantly more beneficial to spend time with that people. It is not appropriate to make changes to the life of another person; but, it is possible to admire their work or art, as he exhibits by viewing all of the performances twice or three times. Not even he is aware of his own identity.

He went shopping for himself as well as for Manya, paying special attention to the requirements that she had specifically. He noticed that she did not bring any shoes that were comfy, so he picked for her a pair of shoes. He doesn't show any appreciation for her, she always manages to misplace her earphone. In addition to a few garments due to the atmosphere. The temperature was quite chilly, which was strange for Manya because she normally lives in Mumbai, where the weather is often changing. Manya would have expected the weather to be warmer.

❧❧❧

Manya leaped straight into the bed because she was unable to withstand the cold and she couldn't stand it. They both had the most sluggish birthdays in the history of the world. They contemplated a great deal of things, but they were unable to leave because of the heavy snowstorm that was covering the ground. Because of the warning, they were unable to leave the building. The one and only happy thing about the situation was that they were able to eat some cake. The candle was lit by her next to the bed. The cake appears to be fresh, at least. Moreover, Danish wrapped himself in the blanket as well. He refuses to remove it, stating that it does not appear attractive in photographs.

While trembling, he extinguished the candles with a blow. He then proceeded to give Manya his initial bite. In conclusion, he did not wait for his own food to arrive. Later, he consumed himself. He chuckles and says, "You watch me eat." Because

Manya has shooting, which will ruin her appearance, she was unable to consume much more food. Because of this, she is required to exert a great deal of control. It was a promise that she made to herself that by the time the movie was over, she would have consumed more food. In point of fact, however, she does not.

"What should we do at this point?" Danish was wanting to know more, but Manya was at a loss for something to say. "If we were to..." They considered celebrating, but found themselves with nothing to do; they were not in the mood for a movie, they did not want to go outdoors, they had already had their drink, and they did not feel like having more. They were unable to rejoice because life had become so monotonous that they had forgotten how to celebrate.

She reached into her pocket and brought out a small box, saying, "Oh, your gift."

He didn't like to acknowledge it, but he enjoys receiving presents. "What is in it?" he asked.

Immediately after putting it on, he proclaimed, "It's a bracelet," and then proceeded to display it.

Despite the fact that it was painful for him, he had to give up his blanket in order to give her a gift. He asked her, "It's not my birthday; why are you giving me a gift?" She told him that she would not accept the gift. "You have no choice; these things are not going to fit me," he remarked as he threw the box right into her hands. "I have no other choice." He doesn't give it much thought, but he was concerned about the possibility that she wouldn't like it. In spite of this, she was taken aback by the unexpected acts that he took. The question was interpreted incorrectly by her. "Do you believe that I don't wear nice clothes?" The response was a resounding "No."

"I know, I was trying to trigger you," she smiled, but he glared at her. Still, he can smile, and that is what makes him happy. Perhaps she likes it. They both roll their eyes at what they should do next; there is no plan. She felt a little guilty that she couldn't do much for his birthday, but she thought about doing it after some time had passed. At least she made one promise: during his birthday, she will be there to celebrate with him.

A spontaneous reaction from Danish was when came closer, "One kiss won't ruin our friendship, right?" However, he did not shy away from the situation because he already had a lot of struggles. "The thought of it already destroys you." He couldn't have asked for anything more to bring her closer to him. He held her head and gently rubbed her hair. She asked. But he kisses her first. The other hand goes to the waist. She kisses back. Both of them could hear their hearts thumping. A few minutes before, they don't have a plan, but they forget about everything. Instead, they know only each other. It felt like a sense of relief that, after so many years, he could feel that she was for him and that he was for her.

And so on.

Has it been 17 hours since he ended their 25-year friendship to become a boyfriend, a milestone he has been counting since their birth? That feeling is insane for him. He couldn't hide his happiness. "What's the matter? How can you be so happy on this type of vacation?" The constant planning and omission of work left Sanvi exhausted. She was so tired that she barely slept. He hesitated to tell her because he knew she would have a dramatic reaction. He just smiles; that's all he knows. "Forget it; where is Manya? It's getting late." In a moment, she entered the restaurant. She made a hasty peek around the dining area and became aware of their presence. She leaped forward to meet Danish's cheeks with a kiss. Sanvi was completely awestruck over them.

"Just what!!!!!!"

Her life has been filled with so many experiences that she is no longer surprised by anything. "I found this to be an extremely peculiar occurrence." Initially, she was under the impression that it was a humorous joke. However, things appear to be different now. Nevertheless, it is not as if it will never occur; she was aware that at some point in the future, they will develop into a possessive pair. Her sole fear is that she is not dating an actor. This is the one thing that worries her.

"What's the matter with your response?" Manya glared at her with a growl.

She responded, "You're asking me this; anyone who sees you will get shocked; just look at yourself," while hiding her lips since she was embarrassed. They lowered their voices when they recalled that they were in a public place. Nevertheless, they made a lot of noise.

The Danish never set foot behind the scenes of a movie. It was not in his mind that there would be such a large number of people. On the other hand, he quickly comes to the conclusion that seeing the films being made is an extremely tedious experience. It is highly likely that you will find the procedure annoying and uninteresting, even if you have a strong interest in filmmaking. Over the course of nearly two hours, they were practicing the same scene, but there were occasions when the background was either dull or excessively bright. They were waiting for a clean sky to appear in the interim. The procedure took a very long time. Despite this, he continues to watch there continuously, not even taking a single time off. He promised that he would take a day off for himself, and he kept his word.

He sat there impatiently waiting for Manya, with the expectation that once she was liberated, they would run away from the scene. That being said, Manya was not having a good time because she was attempting to put her all energy to the situation. Finding it difficult to embody a genuine personality was something she was struggling with. Her thoughts were going to be with Danish. The fact that she was obligated to fulfil the terms of her contract, however, rendered it impossible for her to refuse her task. She was, nevertheless, giving it her best.

Every single member of the crew was sick of the weather. The second time around, they sat down in the hope of gaining a better view. Despite the fact that Manya was unable to explain herself due to the presence of everyone else, she was still able to give him the most charming smile. This was despite the fact that she only had a brief opportunity to spend time with him while he was present. It is then that he remarks, "Your profession appears to be challenging," but he has lost his point. "It's only the second day, and you're already losing it," she said to him as she patted him on the shoulder. Their faces were illuminated by the icy breeze, which felt like a burst of light. That was a welcome change. There was only one point of view maintained by Danish to Manya. He could spend the entire day gazing at her and admiring her. Truly, all he wants to do is give you a hug. The act of cuddling. There is no limit to what can be accomplished, but it must be for her gain. She tells him, "You can see other things as well," while positioning his cheeks to the opposite side of his face. When asked about it, he maintained his consistency by replying, "I can't do anything; now I cannot see either, that's mean."

When Danish want to kiss, they move forward. The statement that she made was, "You are demanding," but she also came forward. On the other hand, she was going to push him back. A deluge of water, on the other hand, struck them. It was not disorienting; rather, it was similar to a waterfall. If you are out in the open for even five seconds, your clothes will become soaked. The technological devices that everyone owns ought to be preserved. Within a split second, the entire shooting scene was completely obliterated. However, Danish did not let this deter him; in order to flee the scene, he took Manya's hand and quickly ran away. Over the course of so many years, he waited for the opportunity for them to be together. Despite the fact that they have been together for a considerable amount of time, this one felt very different from the others.

Sanvi made an effort to approach her. On the other hand, they had already left; she did not even include her phone in her luggage. Numerous months later, Manya broke into a gleeful smile. "Yet, where are we going to go?" They weren't in any exotic or luxurious places. But they realize it isn't the place; it's the people. They didn't have a plan, so they decided to take a bus. Which was best for the mountain? They were watching the rain. "You can get cool." He tossed her around in order to guarantee that it dried. Beginning when she was a child, she has always had a fever whenever she does not brush her hair. The alternative was for her to press her head against his jacket.

"I am not the one who took my bag."

"Don't be concerned, I have my phone with me."

"All right"

Even though there was a significant amount of rain, the director was still hoping to shoot. Despite the fact that he did not permit anyone to leave, he was not aware that the principal actress was not participating. Nevertheless, Manya was unconcerned about that. Because they had no other choice, they decided to celebrate in the rain, despite the fact that it was not a particularly nice experience. In situations where it has been a while since you have loved life, even the little things can bring you joy.

Danish was concerned that Manya would come down with an illness because she had a commitment at work. In light of this, they decided to get off the bus and have a Desi Chinese, which is yet another type of cuisine that India has developed. The greatest place to eat noodles was next to the fire, which they craved.

"It still bothers me to think that if we were together, would we get along well, or is what we are currently doing right?" Manya reminds him of a period when she always knew Danish's feelings, but she never wanted to upset him. She was always aware of what he was going through. A lot of feelings were never entirely clear. Even though she was aware that they would be the greatest of friends forever, she must remember to grow up and think rationally. Because of the distance, they were apprehensive. As time passes, not only do locations change, but so do thoughts, minds, and preferences. The truth is that we are always the same on the inside. "I was genuinely hurt by your emotional investment in me, and I felt like a poor friend. I'll never forget how you were crying that night when I had an accident; you didn't show up, but I woke up in the middle of the night because of you. I was deeply hurt by your emotional investment in me. When I hear you, I am reminded of a period when he was crying in a sincere way." Despite the fact that he believed she had not discovered it, this is not the case. Aware of their genuine intents, he chuckled at their silly deeds and laughed at their foolishness.

Then, she leaned her head against his shoulder. Her father, who had always thought that she would be alone in life like him, was the person she believed would be able to assist her in finding someone to share her life with. In a proud tone, he stated, "Your father has always been aware of both you and me." Manya was so taken aback that she reached out and grabbed his cheeks, asking, "Really?" She experienced a little sense of comfort, but it was still a blow to her. "I never felt the need for family when I was with my dad; I didn't have any siblings, but I was happy; no one would annoy me, but now I feel so lonely." In spite of the fact that I question myself, my comprehension continues to be elusive.

Putting her head on his shoulder, he comforted her by saying, "You are not alone." Taking her into his arms, he pressed her. "That is way too cool.

In spite of the fact that the weather was terrible, Manya was unable to get her hands on a cake. Despite the fact that Danish did not want to eat more cake, she did not find the location to be particularly appealing, and she did not receive any assistance from him. Being happy brought him a sense of fulfilment. After trying all of the street food, which, given the rainy weather, had the potential to make them sick, they made their way to the hotel. After entering the hotel, they made their way to the room; however, Manya chose to go in a different direction. As well as him to pool. Wishing him a happy birthday, everyone is getting up to applaud him. Joy overtook him despite the fact that it was an embarrassing situation. The banner that he was holding stated, "YOU ARE THE BEST BOYFRIEND." "I found it to be quite corny." He stood there holding the banner. It made him laugh, which prompted him to inquire, "What is this?"

Dance was something that everyone wanted to do, but Danish was apprehensive. In order to imitate his simplistic dancing move, they made the decision. The fact that everyone followed suit, on the other hand, was a pleasant sight. What happened to the cake?

In addition, they did not receive the cake since the personnel at the hotel was uncertain about its availability. "It's fine; I don't want cake." Manya found comedy in the fact that she never received the cake on time, despite the fact that she felt ashamed. However, that is not a problem because they are together.

"How are you able to treat me in such a manner? You are lying to me"

"It was because I was hesitant that I was unable to say anything"

"Wow, what a silly excuse is that?"

"I am not going to keep anything from you because you are not my girlfriend"

"Oh, that's definitely painful."

It came as a surprise to the friends of Danish when the information of his girlfriend reveal. They maintained a steady level of trust in his claims and accepted everything that he stated. His presentation of everything was plain, and he was a man who was also obedient. Despite this, he continued to make an attempt to connect with everyone, even after he had relocated to India. in order to avoid damage to relationships with other people. Making an effort to live a life that is balanced. Never in his wildest dreams did he expect that his friends would be able to get updates via the internet. "Okay, a serious question: do you get married or is this all just a coincidence?" In response to the question, Danish laughed and remarked, "I don't do causal things with people I love." It was his buddies that considered his comments to be flattering. When one of his friends indicated seriousness, he answered by saying, "Actually, you should; you both seem happy." He had always been a jokester and a fun person, but this time he responded appropriately. Danish flashed a grin.

When my Danish buddy saw reflection of Manya on his laptop screen, he was taken aback. Both of them had returned to their respective places of employment. Due to the fact that he was a tremendous fan of hers, she was keeping a special premiere ticket out for him! In the end, they were never able to meet. He couldn't believe that he was able to shed tears at that precise moment. It was Danish who yelled out "Control." His friend was so ecstatic that he felt the need to embrace her. Due to the fact that the hug was taking an excessive amount of time, Danish made the decision to separate them because he saw this as his opportunity.

"You have such a stunning appearance"

"Yeah, I know," Danish could not possibly disagree with him.

The words came out of his mouth as he continued to hold her hand "I just love your show"

"Whoa, my goodness! To my surprise, I was unaware that you were such a huge fan"

The only thing that Manya did was laugh and smile; she had no idea that it would one day people become her fans. She was mainly concerned with her adversaries. On the other hand, she was maturing steadily with each passing day. Together, they make their home in India. Manya was compelled to go back to the United States as part of an agreement that Danish and Manya signed verbally. However, Danish is required to return because of this arrangement. A period of two years has passed since the beginning of their relationship. Because he had made such a significant sacrifice, she was strange. He need him to come back. Everything worked out to be a positive outcome. The only idea that Danish had of her was that they were a married pair. Despite this, Danish declared his intention to marry her during their first date together. However, he continued to have the desire to devote a greater amount of time to Manya schooling herself. She is curious about gaining a great deal of knowledge. In order to maintain mental steadiness. The state of being mature. They are successful at communicating with one another. For the purpose of maintaining communication, the Danish have always believed that they would fight a great deal, although in reality, they hardly ever do so. They either go on a journey together, she pays him a visit, or he pays her a visit. The reason that security is able to identify her is because she has visited his workplace on numerous occasions. Also, invite her to come.

It is early in the morning for the Danish. He was packing. After that, he went alongside her. Manya took the time to greet everyone. "You're not ready to marry me, yet you keep showing up at the office." In response to his inquiry, Manya has returned. "Are you experiencing any difficulties?"

"Definitely not at all"

"As a matter of fact, I never really have the impression that I need to get married since I always have the impression that I am already one. To me, it is nothing more than a set of regulations prescribed by society; nonetheless, I do enjoy wearing such costumes and participating in celebrations."

It is a flight that they have catch up. "Just let go."

A flight to India was scheduled for them. In terms of the time, Danish was incorrect, but Manya, fortunately, was correct. Due to the fact that they hadn't sat down together in quite some time, they made the decision to meet Danish's parents. In order to pick them up, Sanvi arrived. "What a long time it has been. Just a regular boy." However, she did not miss him at all because he was always distinct from her. She actually missed Danish food. Neither one of them can wait to get back to their own place. After such a long travel, they need to take some time to rest and get some fresh air. The parents of Danish reside in a different location. "Why are you so well dressed?" His parents were dressed in traditional garb, which came as a surprise to Danish. For what reason is he curious? At the same time, Manya hurriedly prepared herself for the situation. Sanvi yelled at him the following: "You should also get ready; we only have time for eleven o'clock in the morning." Despite the fact that Manya was wearing a plain saree, she now seemed to have grown up. It works well for her.

Upon receiving his garments, Danish did not take them with him but instead inquired about them with Manya. "If you wanted a marriage, then I will do all in my possibility to get one as quickly as I possibly can. Yesterday, you inquired, and I am responding with a positive answer today." It came as a complete surprise to Danish that his parents had consented to this. "Now, please put on some clothes; we have some time."

In order to have a conversation, Manya welcomed him inside the room. "I am aware that it is exceedingly quick, but I would like to register right away. You are free to choose when you should put on those cumbersome traditional garments, all right?" Suddenly, she burst out laughing when he kissed her five times at once. The two of them held each other. "Despite the fact that you didn't have to be in a rush, I just adore it." He comes to a halt in the centre.

"I know you love him and you love her, but the court won't wait for you guys to hurry," Sanvi shouted as she dragged them to the car. "So hurry up!"

Danish and Manya were experiencing a great deal of anxiety. They were supported by his parents, and their voyage is going to be filled with wonderful moments. "What is the reason for you making it so challenging?" The response that Sanvi gave to the query was that it was nothing more than a registration. Manya, on the other hand, increases her voice in an effort to calm her down. In an effort to make their lives more lovely and better, the two of them are holding hands here. They do not engage in conflict; rather, they support one another, without exception. "It's so terrible!" Sanvi was left in awe as she watched them exchange vows.

The registrar was exhausted, but they had a lot of energy with them when they received the call. Following the signing of Manya came the signing of Danish. Their parents presented them with a flower mala, which provided a touch of realism to the situation. "Okay, here's a picture."

They went for a family photograph proceeding to couple photos.